Sweet Farm of Mine

by

Candace A. Hennekens

Other Books by Candace A. Hennekens

Sweet Land of Mine, electronic and print versions

Healing Your Life: Recovery from Domestic Abuse, electronic and print versions

Yes to Career Success! For Women in Transition, print version

There's a Rainbow in My Glass of Lemonade, electronic version

Melpomene's Hand, electronic version

Warm Stanchions and Red Barns with Blue Roofs, electronic and print versions

Healing Your Life: Recovery from Domestic Abuse with Free Bonus There's a Rainbow in my Glass of Lemonade, electronic version

Women of the Farm: Five Short Stories, electronic version

Cream from Butterflies, electronic version

Samantha Says, electronic version

Dedication

Norb, this one's for you

Table of Contents

Preface

Thousands of years ago the great glacier moved over the state of Wisconsin, carving out hills and valleys, creating lakes big and small, melting into rivers, long and short, leaving its imprint behind. In the middle of one of those valleys that at first seems flat but which gently undulates into tree-covered hills, there is a farm.

The view from the farm is of the hills. In winter, evergreens and bare trunks are dusted with white snow and sparkling hoarfrost. In spring, deciduous trees send out tender shoots in delicate shades of pink, yellow and fragile green, then ripen to join the darker greens of pine, spruce and fir and color the hills with all the rich shades of green's possibility— viridian, sap, olive, jade, emerald, hooker's—as they leaf out thickly. In autumn the hills flame into tawny gold, brocade red, russet brown and bright yellow.

Standing in the fields on the farm, your eyes roam the hills, imagining what lies beneath the trees, what has transpired in other times, before man existed on the land, when the Indians roamed, when the loggers harvested, before the farmers came to claim the land. Now the imprint of the farmer is on the land—waving fields of corn and soybeans, lush pastures of grasses, alfalfa and clover.

Farm buildings dot the valley—red barns with blue roofs, white wooden corn cribs, sheds in gun metal gray or brick red, black and white dairy cows, brown beef cattle, and white houses that stand apart from farm buildings. From a distance, none of the work and worry of farming is visible, only the neat orderly arrangement of the buildings, fields, and pastures.

Not far from a state highway, taking a county road, then following another country road, you'll turn onto a long straight driveway. You will travel under a bower of tall stately trees that have been standing as sentinels for almost a hundred years. If it's winter, the oaks will have leaves clinging stubbornly to the gnarly branches. Birds will be fluttering in the pine and spruce branches. In spring, oak, locust and maple leaf into green garments, forming a tunnel to the private world of the farm.

All farms, big or small, are worlds unto themselves, showing the intricacies of daily life only to the inhabitants, who, over time, take the cycles, the seasons, the good times and the bad, into the core of their being until they become at one with their farm.

Chapter One
Taking the Leap

It was a cold January afternoon. My father Arlan and I had finished touring old Charlie's farm on the outskirts of Rush River, a small town in northwest Wisconsin. We had looked over the house, inspected the barn and outbuildings. The buildings were weathered, paint long gone, but a patch of barn red or white still clung stubbornly to the silver gray wood. Our assessment was that useful life was left in the buildings. Their support timbers stood tall, hewn from trees cut to clear the land for this farm.

"Ruth," my father pointed out, "see the mortise and tenon joints, wooden pegs instead of nails?"

Once we started looking, construction methods from days gone by became more and more fascinating. Charlie could point to the different timbers and tell what they were made from. "This one's a tamarack," he'd say. "Here's an oak. My grandfather and father built all these buildings. My grandfather came over from Germany after my grandmother died. He traveled with his youngest son, that was my father, on a ship to Canada, then they found their way to Wisconsin to work in the lumber business. After they'd made some money, they bought this farm. My father married my mother, who had been born in this country, but her parents had emigrated from France. My grandfather lived with my parents until his death. I was a boy when he died but old enough to remember him."

Now we headed to the house. Charlie was cold, and wanted a cup of coffee. The house and one of the sheds were the only buildings with white paint. The house was a big two story square house with a wide front porch, topped by a capacious upstairs attic with windows that looked out in all four directions. Charlie told us proudly that he had painted the house himself eight years ago. Watching the way he shuffled when he walked, it was hard to believe that he had been able to climb a ladder. Charlie explained how the house had been shipped on the railroad to Rush River. His grandfather and his father had bought it from the Sears catalog, and had assembled it piece by piece.

"After the house was finished, my grandfather retired to his rocking chair. In the warm months, he sat on the front porch. When it got cold, he moved his chair to the kitchen. I never heard my mother complain about my grandfather, though he was a crusty old curmudgeon, German through and through, as stubborn as they come. Have you heard this one Ruth? You can always tell a German but you can't tell them much?" Charlie guffawed when he finished, pleased with his own humor.

I chuckled. I cocked my head in the direction of Arlan. "He's German, Charlie. I do believe you've pegged him."

Now my father chuckled. "But don't forget Ruthie," he said to me, "you're half German. The other half is French. That's where you get your hot head, from the French side of the family."

We three—Charlie, my father, and I— sat down to make a deal. My father calls me Ruthie. My mother and father named me Ruth because it was a name from the Bible. It was a good name and my mother hoped I would live up to it. When my mother said my name, "Ruth", her lips formed a heart and she mouthed my name lovingly as sound escaped from her lips.

I was a good child, but as a teenager became overly curious, searching out the depths of life, anxious to drink coffee, read poetry, smoke cigarettes and whatever else was available, while discussing the meaning of life. After those long sessions getting at its meaning, you would think I would have found some. But I was still the lost curious child.

My mother stopped forming her lips into a heart after I grew up. She chided me with her voice, "Ruth", she would say sharply, when she disapproved. The gulf between us widened. When we talked, she asked if my husband Rich and I were getting along. At first, I would be surprised by her question. Later, I realized that she was wondering when the little ones were going to come.

Now my mother was gone, leaving my father to find his way alone. My father had been a decade older than she. They had never dreamed she would die first. My father had always soothed her, "You'll never die, and I will live forever." Now he was a lost man without her. We had that in common—being lost.

I had been gone fourteen years and my life away had been different from my Midwest upbringing. In California I had been a hard driving business executive, working long hours, and indulging in luxuries. I married an attorney, and he worked even longer hours. My husband Rich had never wanted children, a piece of information I had learned in my late twenties when I head the loud ticking of my biological clock. To me having a family had been so much a given that I had never brought up the subject for discussion during our courtship days or early years of marriage. Rich was adamant. His childhood had been unhappy. I suspected abuse, but he would never say one way or the other. I resigned myself to a marriage without children. My attempts to sublimate, to channel maternal energy into my career had worked for awhile, but around the age of thirty, I started questioning everything about my life.

I had heard that turning thirty is harder for a woman than a man. For men forty was their mid-life crisis. When I couldn't quell the desire for nurturing any longer, I asked for a divorce. I hoped doing so would bring Rich around. To my surprise, he agreed. We parted as amicably as two people married a decade with a major difference between them could manage. It seemed like a good idea to move back home, to help my father, and put some distance between Rich and me. I felt burned out by life. I didn't know what I wanted to do, and my father's plans intrigued me.

My father sold the big old house where I had grown up. I joined him in an apartment, and we began looking for a farm. A former customer gave him the tip about Charlie's farm. My father had sold seed corn, alfalfa and liquid fertilizer for a family-owned seed company for thirty years. He had retired a few months before my mother's sudden death. She had been an educator, principal at the grade school where I'd gone as a child.

The idea to buy a farm was something my father had seized a few months after my mother's death. When he brought the idea up for discussion, I remembered back to childhood, how he hankered for a farm even then. But my mother was a city girl and wouldn't hear of it.

We kids, my older brother and my two younger sisters, and I had tried talking him out of the plan, but he wouldn't listen. During my divorce, the idea to come back and help him had come to me one evening when I worked in the yard. Rich wouldn't eat vegetables. We gardened in perennials, big beds of roses, and specimen plants of different varieties. I loved the garden and spent my evening working there when I arrived home to an empty house. I'd work until dark, then make dinner, and finally Rich would come dragging in the door. He was a criminal lawyer and was often so preoccupied that I felt like another shadow in the house. I was beginning to realize how lonely I had felt during my marriage now that I had my father as a companion.

We were sitting at the small round table where Charlie had eaten his meals for decades. Charlie would know about loneliness. He had lived alone on this farm for more than thirty years. I could see from the stilted way he held his body, the careful way he searched for words, that he had grown accustomed to life alone. Now being with people seemed foreign to him. He had forgotten about human contact.

My father had been lonely. When I brought up the idea of coming back to Wisconsin to join him in the venture, he hadn't tried to talk me out of it. At first, I was floating a trial balloon, but before I knew it, my father had surrounded it with hopes and dreams, then firmly made plans. I was swept into the venture before I'd really had time to think about it.

I had been saying to myself, when doubts about what I was doing surfaced, that I had to do something. Farming didn't seem like such an outlandish idea when I was in California. Back there, it has been a warm fuzzy, something to hug when I felt lost and alone. But once I was home, I wondered if this was what I should do.

In a way, it was almost too late. To back out now would disappoint my father. I didn't want to disappoint him. If nothing else, going into the venture would buy me some time while I figured out what I really wanted to do.

My father's relief at having company made him easy to come home to. He didn't probe about my divorce from Rich. For my father, divorce would have been unimaginable. He would have stuck it out. He was that kind of man. He would have stuck it out and somehow he would have made the marriage work.

I didn't tell him that it was not being alone that made you lonely. You could be alone and married. I shocked my siblings when I turned up at my father's doorstep a few months ago. My brother and two sisters couldn't believe I had walked away, leaving behind most of what I owned. They had imagined all those years that I had the perfect life. But when I told them Rich wanted to remain childless, they softened. My brother had three children, teenagers now, and my two younger sisters had two children each. Their lives revolved around their children so they seemed to understand.

In front of my father were the soil maps for the farm. My father was hunkered over them, studying the different soil types, mouthing words that sounded like foreign countries to me, Vesper, Ludington, and Friendship. Learning soil types wasn't the only challenge ahead of me.

Even though I blamed the divorce on Rich, I was beginning to see that there was more than not wanting children. I hadn't realized what I hadn't had until I was back home. The down-home feeling you get when you hang around with Midwesterners felt comfortable. They are not people who want immaculate, exquisitely decorated homes, and yards that look like golf courses. They believe in family and hard work. Little League, ballet and piano recitals, PTA meetings, family reunions, these outings are the basis for their social life, not expensive dinners at fancy restaurants, and exotic vacation cruises every year on your wedding anniversary. They were down to earth, in touch with what really mattered in life. I'd also missed the changing beauty of Wisconsin. I missed the woods, lakes, rivers, and hills. Once I was back home, I realized I'd stayed away too long from a world intrinsic to my well being. I missed little from my old life, yet at the same time I wasn't sure what I wanted in this new one.

In that moment before the three of us got down to business, while we were eating Windmill cookies and drinking dark strong coffee from thick china cups that were almost as old as Charlie, there was a pause. In the swinging of the pendulum on a grandfather clock, there is a pause when the pendulum reverses direction, a momentary stopping of action while inertia works against the change.

I was in the pause. It was not too late to stop action. I could still cast my eyes down to my lap, and not meet my father's gaze. I could say, "We need to think about this."

Our chairs would scrape back. We would push ourselves up to say a few awkward words of farewell to Charlie, and then my father and I would get into our car. As we departed, I would have to face my father's wrath. He would calm down eventually, he would finally understand. Maybe he would go forward without me.

I twisted the cup around in my hand. Hairline cracks ran from the bottom to the lip, and as I brought the cup to my mouth to sip the coffee, I felt as if I were watching myself in a movie. Just like the cracks in the cup, ready to split open under the right pressure, I could see my life, ready to be split apart. All I had to do was nod my head, give some indication that I was going to go through with the deal, going to be my father's partner, and my life would split wide open.

But I couldn't fool myself. The cracks had been forming, growing, becoming bigger, darker, deeper as I lived out my years on this earth. My life was already split apart. Leaving Rich had left me with money but very little else. I had my brains, my health, and my father. I had this plan to be a farmer. Anything else I couldn't claim.

Farming was risky, but I was playing for higher stakes than whether or not I could make myself into a farmer. I needed to find myself. I watched my father as he sat there, pipe in hand, legs crossed, drawing out the old man. My father had coaxed, wheedled and finessed old Charlie to make this moment happen. My father knew what he wanted.

Other potential buyers were beating on the doors of Charlie's house, trying to make him sell the farm. Some wanted the house. It was a beautiful old home that needed a woman's touch again. Charlie's mother had planted the yard with lilacs, rose bushes, grape vines, apple, pear, and plum trees. Some wanted the land to subdivide for building lots. That's something my husband Rich would have done, bought an old farm and then torn all the buildings down, leaving vestiges of the landscaping to make the new houses seem less obtrusive on the fertile farm land.

We had told Charlie about our plans to raise beef cattle. The farm had good soil, and would grow corn, soybeans, hay and oats, feed for cattle. If every year you gave back to the land what it had given you, you could farm here forever. That's what my father had been telling me. We could own 240 acres of valuable farmland if we made an offer.

My father had been telling me that in a sense we were going back in time. "Farms are either going to become big operations, hundreds of acres to carry the debt load, or they're going to get sliced into smaller hobby farms. What I propose is that we try to be smart about our debt. That way we'll be able to buy the farm and live in one of the most beautiful parts of the state, without the worry of owing money to the bank."

I was closer to thirty-five than thirty. My former husband's words rang in my head. "Ruth, you can't go home again. You have to move on," he said to me as he watched me pack the few possessions I was taking. When I said goodbye to him and climbed into my car, he came running, his hands full of things. "Ruth, these are yours too. Take them," he said, thrusting pictures, cut crystal and candle holders into my lap. "Don't you want them?" he asked me, as I accepted them reluctantly.

"I never wanted any of that," I said to him.

"What are you talking about Ruth?" he said, looking surprised and hurt. "We picked these things out together."

"I want a family, Rich. I want a family."

"But you and I are a family, Ruth. You and I are a family even if we don't have children."

"You might think so Rich, but I don't. We were two people leading separate lives, living in the same house without warmth. I want a real marriage. I want children. And now it may be too late for that."

"Now you're being dramatic, Ruth. Don't be ridiculous. You're still young. You can bear children. You don't need a husband to have children. Go to a sperm bank. You can have all the children you want."

"There's no need to be cruel, Rich," I cried in pain.

Then I felt like being cruel. "You would have made a poor father anyway. You'd be at the office everyday, you'd never see them. They would be in bed before you got home."

"I never heard you complain about the money I brought home to enjoy," Rich retorted.

I stopped myself before I said anything more. "Well, it's all yours now," I said.

He shook his head, and held up his hand to silence me. "Go home," he said. "You'll be fine once you get your bearings." He opened his pocket and pulled out a check. My eyes opened wide when I saw what he'd made it out for. "I'll give you the settlement now. So you have some money to make a fresh start. I've never been stingy with you, and I don't want to hear you ever say that about me to anyone. I was good to you Ruth. I gave you what I thought you wanted. I never knew children mattered that much to you."

"Would it have made any difference to you? Would you have changed your mind?" I asked him.

"Probably not," he answered. He turned and walked away.

I drove cross-country in three days.

At this moment, I could change my mind. The pendulum had stopped while it fought inertia. But when I reached across the table for the business card of Charlie's attorney, I would be committed.

What hung in the air was fear. I could almost smell it. Fear to create the life I wanted. But this was crazy, I thought to myself, to buy a farm, "a farm", I would say aloud, as if it were a country I had never visited.

Everything was on the line.

The one person who understood my need to connect with something real, fundamental and solid was the only person I would disappoint if I backed out.

If I had ever had any illusions of control over life, I knew they didn't exist in farming. Farming is about weather. Rains that fall without mercy so that seed rots in the ground. Hot dry spells that come when the corn needs rain to grow fat kernels. Frosts that kill before soybeans have matured. I may have lived in a city for the last fourteen years, but I had grown up listening to talk about farming.

If you're lucky and get a good crop, then you may not receive a fair price, a price that compensates you for your inputs and gives you a profit. Farmers in Brazil compete with farmers in Wisconsin. Just when you get a bumper crop, the bottom drops out of the market.

And who was I to think I could farm anyway? Farmers grow up on farms. Farmers are men. Farmers are not college-educated businesswomen who have no idea what they're getting into.

There was an alternative. I could take another job. Find another husband. No one would blame me. My father would understand. In talking out our plan, my father had emphasized that it had to be my decision. He wasn't going to make me do this.

He was hoping I would do it, but in the end, when all was said and done, he could just as easily reach across the table and take the card from Charlie and farm without me. He said he didn't really need me. He was still strong, still vital. He had money. He could act alone.

I knew what my father couldn't acknowledge. His roots came from the land. Years ago he had wanted to farm. But he had been afraid. Too much risk. He would have had to move off the farm where he grew up and buy his own. Start from scratch. He came from a big family. The eldest son took over the family farm. It wasn't big enough for more than one son. My father had been left in the cold. When he married, my mother opposed any plans of farming. He would have had to fight her.

He had been me at one time. The issue hadn't been children; it had been farming.

Maybe, for all his bluff about how it would work out, he needed me. We needed each other.

I asked myself, "Is this what I want?"

Then I watched my hand reach across the table. Charlie started to hand me the business card but he stopped. "I'm curious," he said, "why such a lovely young woman as you would want to be a farmer. It's hard work. It's dirty work. Driving tractor in the hot sun makes wrinkles on your face. You farm long enough and your back aches all the time, your hands are callused and hard. What do you know about farming anyway?"

I shrugged my shoulders. "Nothing," I said.

"Well then tell me why you want to be a farmer?"

I met his gaze. His blue eyes were steady. They didn't look away from mine. He was waiting patiently for an answer.

"I don't know what else to do. I'm divorced. I'm tired of the work I did back in California. I like gardening. It's a chance to do something with my father. Make a new start. Why not?"

"I don't know," Charlie said, "that doesn't seem like a strong reason. Have you ever touched a beef cow?"

"No," I responded.

"Do you know what corn looks like?"

"I grew up in Wisconsin. Of course I know what corn looks like."

"Well, have you ever planted any?"

"I've gardened. I picked corn when I was kid. I de-tasseled seed corn when I was in high school. Busload of kids were hired to de-tassel corn. It was fun."

Charlie's blue eyes were watching me. I dropped my eyes down to my lap. "You're like all the others. You think I'm crazy."

In the silence that followed, Charlie slowly got up and brought the coffee pot back to the table. "Can I warm yours?" he asked.

I shook my head no.

He filled his cup and shuffled back to put the pot back on the burner, then came back to the table and sat down heavily.

"You know farming is a privilege, don't you? You are a steward of the land. It's not about running the plow up and down the rows, spraying at the right time. It's about falling into the rhythm of the land, listening to what it tells you. You can learn what you need to know to be a farmer, but you got to have that special feeling about land and animals to be a success. Tell me something that would make me think you would be a good farmer."

I looked up. Charlie was still waiting for my answer. I thought a minute. Then I spoke. "I had everything anyone could want back in California. My husband was a successful attorney. I worked for a big insurance agency and made a lot of money myself. We had a new four-bedroom house. We had new furniture. I wore the most expensive clothes. I bought a new car every year. But everything I had was a thing. I didn't have roots. It was follow the big money wherever it takes you. I didn't have my heart in my life. It was how fast I could make money. And after awhile, you start to figure out that money can't buy you satisfaction. I can tell you this much. The view of the hills soothes my soul. The feel of soil on my fingers is better than a big diamond on my hand. The taste of fresh vegetables right from the earth is better than eating at a fancy restaurant. I'm smart and I can learn anything I set my mind to learn. I want to see if this is where I belong. I don't know if I'll be a good farmer, but I will promise you this much, I will give it everything I've got."

Again there was silence. Charlie reached into his shirt pocket and pulled a card out. He handed it to me. It was his attorney's business card.

"We'll contact your attorney first thing Monday morning. Does he know what you want?' I asked.

Charlie's blue eyes met my gaze. "You know retirement living doesn't come cheap, Ruth. Everything I have is tied up in the farm, but I think we can work out a deal."

I pushed my chair back. Charlie and Arlan followed suit. We rounded up our coats, and shook hands. Charlie turned my hand over. "I'm going to take a good look at your hand because it won't be long before it will be covered with calluses." Then he smiled at me. "That's not a bad thing, Ruth. It just means you know what hard work is all about."

We rode in silence most of the way to the small apartment we called home. The sun had disappeared behind clouds and the January landscape seemed harsh and bleak. I felt unsettled, not as sure of my decision as I led Charlie to believe, but I kept this to myself. My father cleared his throat several times then spoke.

"That was a fine answer you gave, Ruthie. I'm not telling you it's going to be easy. Real satisfaction doesn't come from doing what's easy." Then a long pause. He cleared his throat again, twisting his hat in his long bony fingers. "Ruthie, thank you for doing this." He said the words so softly I almost couldn't hear them. Then he turned his face towards the window. We drove the rest of the way in silence.

Chapter Two
Our Friendship Begins

Charlie called early this morning and asked us to come look at some things. He was watching out the front window, waiting for us to arrive. His blue and white striped bib overalls showed though the lace curtains. By the time we got to the back door, he had pulled on an overcoat and black rubber boots that he hadn't bothered to zip. We went back outside. He pointed to the northwest corner of the farm.

"There's a grove of old trees back there, oaks, maple, a few walnuts. Lots of firewood lying around." He gestured to the northeast side of the farm. " That's the best field. Eighty acres of level ground. Grows good corn, I'll tell you."

Then he waved to the southeast corner. "Spring down there. Clean sweet water. I put the calves down there in the summer, and the dry cows too. Good pasture for young heifers. The middle eighty is hay ground; there's some wet spots in spring but clover grows thick and sweet in summer."

He motioned to the southwest. "Heavy wet ground I worked last. The furthest piece gets real wet in the spring, but I never had a year I couldn't plant eventually. I planted soybeans there, and corn, alternately, like the other fields.

Used to plant only corn, but nowadays, soybeans are a good cash crop."

"We hope you'll come visit the farm and give us advice," I said to Charlie.

My father chimed in, "And we'd like your company too."

Charlie seemed not to hear. "Now," he said, "I want to show you a couple of things down the basement."

Charlie shuffled slowly ahead of us, a short stocky man, barrel-chested, the joints in his legs and hips worn down to bone on bone by a lifetime of milking. I noticed Charlie's hands, trembling visibly from the Parkinson's disease that was driving him from the farm. We walked down the steps single file, Charlie in the lead. He was having trouble. We waited patiently behind him as he moved one foot at a time down the steep wooden steps. My father tried to hold his arm but Charlie shook him off.

"Maybe on the way up," he said. Charlie stopped at the bottom, pointing out the washer and dryer. "You can keep those if you want. I won't need them where I'm going."

An old Maytag wringer washer sat there too, next to the laundry sink. The Maytag looked used, but in good condition. The paint was still white and bright red. "Maytag works," Charlie said.

"Looks just like that old Maytag we used to have," my father said. "Your mother loved that old washer. She used it until the wringer broke and parts couldn't be had to fix it. Do you remember how to use it?" he asked me with a smile.

"Well, I was going to ask you the same thing," I said back.

My father chuckled. He already knows that I won't wash his clothes. He says he doesn't care. "You don't think I never washed my own clothes?" he told me. "Who has been taking care of me since your mother died?"

I remember how he washed his clothes when I was a kid. He didn't trust my mother to do it exactly the way he wanted. He wanted his pants hung on the clothesline by the bottoms to dry, the creases in front perfectly aligned. He chided us children if he thought there was too much laundry for my mother, throwing the clothes he deemed still clean into piles on the laundry room floor, making us go down to bring them back to our rooms to hang in the closet. My father always protected my mother from too much work. He knew Saturday chores could overwhelm her.

Then we looked at the root cellar under the front porch, made from bricks with a dirt floor. It was dark, except for the light by the door.

"Potatoes and apples store well here. Good place to go when there's a storm." Charlie pointed to the shelves along one wall. "Those used to be full of my Ma's canning, applesauce, tomatoes, tomato juice, rhubarb, raspberries, grape juice, corn, beans, pickles, jams and jellies of all kinds," he said. "There's a nice fruit orchard out back and the old grape arbor on the side by the clothes lines still produces. It was something my Ma really loved, and we always took care with the fruit trees and grapes. I kept it up even if I didn't can. You'll find varieties of apples you can't buy. There are different kinds of grapes, purple, red, green, with seeds, but good to make jelly."

Charlie stopped talking and his eyes started to twinkle. He looked full of mischief. "You can make wine better than any you got back in California," he said to me. He pronounced California as if it ends in a "ney." This is more evidence of his sense of humor.

Some of the glass jars are light azure blue so I know they're old. In the back, I see some gallon ones, hard to come by, but handy for juice. The newspaper lining the shelves is yellow, falling in pieces to the dirt floor. Cobwebs are thick in the corners.

"You can have the jars too. Won't bring much at the auction and too hard to pack and bring up the steps," Charlie said. We started back up the steps. "Now I'll take some help," he said to my father.

Slowly, laboriously, he lifts one foot to the step and waits for my father to give him a hoist so that he can bring the next foot up. When we make it back upstairs to the kitchen, he is breathing heavily. "I made some coffee," he manages to say, then sits down. "Go ahead and pour some."

I find the china cups in the cupboard and fill them before I sit down. We sit in awkward silence for a while.

"How about a cookie," he asks me. He shows me where they are and I bring the package over to the table.

"What are you going to do with your furniture, Charlie," I ask.

"I've got an auction scheduled for the middle of March. I hope I can last that long. I'm going down hill fast. Might have to move sooner. Got me an apartment at that new place on the other side of town. They cook the meals and you eat in the dining room with the other folks but you've got your own bedroom, and bathroom and living room. My brother helped me find it. It's expensive, I'll tell you that much, but I guess I don't have much choice. No where else for me to go."

"It must feel sad to be leaving the farm after living here all your life," I said.

I am curious about Charlie. I want to know why he never married, how he managed all these years alone. He is something of a recluse, his reputation in town full of mystery, and yet everyone seems to like him.

"Well," Charlie begins, then pauses for what seems a long time. It is as if he is giving the question some serious thought for the first time. He intones his response, "Not really sad so much. More of a relief. It's been hard these last few years. Kind of lonely too. No one to talk to. Some days I don't really feel like cooking for myself but I know I have to. Got to keep eatin' or I'll die for sure. Not much fun anymore either. I've been renting out the land. It just isn't the same when you aren't in charge. I was used to doing it my way, getting the crops in the ground as soon as I could, and making sure I did everything a farmer could do to get a good crop. I'm tired of working all the time. That too. I'd like to rest awhile before I depart for the next life." After each sentence he had paused, as if considering the truth of what to say next.

"We'll be glad to come out and help you pack," my father offers. "We can come out and help you move what you need for your new place."

"I'd sure appreciate that," Charlie says. "It would be a big help. I have to depend on my brother and he isn't much younger than I am. That would be mighty helpful. You got a pickup?"

My father answers Charlie, "Wouldn't be much of a farmer if I didn't have a pickup."

Charlie laughs then, and relaxes some more, his face visibly losing some of its tension. We sit there in silence for awhile, and from a corner somewhere in the house, I hear the ticking of an old clock marking the seconds, while outside the sound of a raucous Blue Jay calling to the clear sky interrupts the quiet of a winter afternoon on a farm.

Chapter Three
Charlie's Auction

The weather on auction day is decent. I feel the enjoyment of being outdoors after a long winter. Charlie's yard is strewn with oak rockers, mattresses, bed frames, headboards, oak dressers, old lamps, desks, sewing machines, and piles of boxes. Though there is some sense of order to the furniture and boxes, it looks as if Charlie has emptied his underwear drawer on the lawn.

Charlie decided not to come to the auction. He called me early this morning. He thought it would be too hard to watch the things he had lived with his entire life leave with strangers. His brother would be there to handle any problems.

The auction is drawing a crowd. The road in front of the farm is getting busy. In order to park, pickups and cars have to hang over the edge of the blacktop, one side of the wheels on the pavement, the other side hanging over the gravel right of way. The slam of truck and car doors sounds like cymbals. Trucks rev their engines as they try to turn around on the road to claim a parking place.

I feel my pulse quicken and an urgency to look over furniture and boxes come over me.

Charlie's solitary existence is part of the draw. Everyone wonders how Charlie managed to live alone. Farming and family are as intertwined as Siamese twins but Charlie had done it alone after his folks passed away. His brothers, except for one who lived in town, had taken up different professions and moved away. Charlie had told me about them. One was a builder. Another welded. A third had moved to Colorado and bought a ranch. Charlie had gotten the farm by default because he never married. He stayed on and then finally, it was all up to him.

I am still thinking of the farm as Charlie's farm. It doesn't seem real that soon my father and I will be in charge. The house seems to stare back from empty windows. I feel a strange mixture of excitement and dread. The bitter taste of stomach acid fills my mouth.

We need to get an auction number. A line has formed going into the kitchen. The auction office has been set up there. My father has left me while he inspects the equipment parked behind the house. I take my place in line. I try to strike up a conversation with the man in front of me, then the woman behind me, but I am ignored.

Next to the line is the food wagon. A turkey roaster sits on the table with bags of hot dogs buns next to it. A half dozen ketchup and mustard bottles, a dish of chopped white onions, a dish of sauerkraut and a dish of sweet pickle relish sit next to the roaster. The smell of hot dogs permeates the air. An urn of coffee sits there too, next to an assortment of dessert bars and cookies. I am tempted by the chocolate chip cookies made with colored M&M's but decide on a bar layered with chocolate chips, maraschino cherries, coconut and nuts on a graham cracker crust. A high school girl working the food table takes my money then hurries to the next customer. The bar is so sweet that the fillings in my teeth ache when I take a bite. By the time I get inside the kitchen, I have eaten the entire bar and it begins forming itself into a hard ball in my churning stomach.

Fred, the auctioneer, is talking to one of the workers but when he sees me he comes over to ask if it is okay to introduce me and my father to the crowd before he starts the auction. I give him my assent, and get a number. When I get outside, I realize that we have never been formally introduced but somehow he knew whom I was.

The crowd had grown while I was in the kitchen. The line is snaking around the house now. Maybe Charlie will get good prices for his things. I can tell that the crowd is a mixture of town and farm folks. There are clusters of farmers standing around in the back by the equipment. They wear caps emblazoned with farm equipment and supplier names—a dark green cap says "Pioneer Seed", another in a lighter shade says, "Nothing runs like a Deere." There are caps in red, blue, yellow, white, sprouting like dandelions on a lawn. Some of the farmers are wearing bib overalls with blue and white stripes like Charlie wears, their jackets stained from barn chores open at the front.

The younger farmers are harder to pick out. They blend better with cleaner clothes, blue jeans and flannel shirts over long underwear that peeks out from the front by the collar. I can tell the farmers by their foreheads that haven't lost the stark whiteness from being shaded by caps when they worked in the sun.

A community of Amish live not far from Rush River. Some have come, tying their horses and neat black buggies away from the crowd, behind the barn. The men wear blue chambray shirts and black trousers and straw hats with black hatbands. They have full beards on their faces. The women wear long black dresses, black hose, black shoes and long black capes and big black hats with wide brims that dip down to cover most of their face and tie under their chins. The Amish stand in a tight knot together, near one of the wagons. They have already claimed a prime spot in front of the auctioneer's stand.

The locals are standing around talking to each other, not interested in what is for sale but in who is here. Most of them are older. The women are bundled up in winter jackets with old silk scarves tied tightly under their chins to keep their heads warm in the light breeze that seems to be coming up. The men stand with their hands in the pockets of their nylon jackets advertising the local bars or businesses on the back.

The sound of their laughter as they swap stories and tell jokes rises up over the soft voices of the women gossiping.

I can spot the serious shoppers by the intensity with which they are pawing through boxes of dishes and miscellaneous items piled on the auction wagons. Two flat wagons are loaded with boxes of things.

Boxes hold old dishes and flat wear, old comforters, sheets and tablecloths, old toys, Christmas decorations, sugar sacks, McCoy vases, a coffee grinder, an antique scale, a bean pot, and a half dozen Red Wing crocks. As the crowd grows, it becomes more difficult to elbow my way to the wagon to look at a box of particular interest.

I look through a box full of old Christmas cards, and pictures. I spot several Native American hand-woven baskets. I lift one up and make out in pencil the price of 75 cents. The basket is in good condition and will bring a hundred times that price, if not more.

I would love to buy everything on the wagon and then take my time going through the boxes, like a long, slow Christmas morning unwrapping hidden delights and treasures.

Out in the yard, bedroom dressers are lined up in a row, bed frames in another, mattresses in another. The dining room table and six leaves in a wooden storage box with the eight matching oak chairs sit next to three old sewing machines, all in wooden cases. I pull up one of the machines, an old Singer with ornate gold filigree on the body. The filigree is worn.

Old wooden oak rockers are clustered together. Potential buyers are sitting on a red velvet chair and couch in nearly new condition. My father and I don't need any of these things, although I would like to try for the dining room table. I go back to study its condition. It needs to be refinished but the box holding the leaves would be handy.

Between the house and the barn is a line up of farm equipment. I wander back there to find my father. He is standing by a Hesston hay stacker, studying its workings. Four sections of drag lie nearby. There's an International 574 tractor, a Case tractor with a loader, a 3-bottom mounted plow, a McCulloch chain saw, some logging chains, a lime spreader, Charlie's 1969 F-250 pick up truck with only 9,000 actual miles on it, and two old washing machines. Someone has dug out the paperwork on the pick up from the glove box. The car was delivered to the Ford dealer in town, back when there was a Ford dealer here. I quickly do some math in my head. Charlie went to town approximately one and a half times a week.

The auctioneer is showing signs of beginning. The crowd starts to form a circle around one of the wagons holding boxes. I go claim a spot. The auctioneer starts tapping and blowing into the microphone. Soon his voice booms out. "Folks, get your numbers now because we'll be starting the auction in a few minutes."

Fred is roly-poly and short, with blond curly hair. He seems to know everyone. He works the crowd, stopping to tease and joke with everyone he sees.

He jumps back onto the wagon. He grabs the microphone and starts teasing one of the old farmers. "Old Roy is here and I don't see Dorothy around anywhere so Roy is going to try to buy it all. Folks, get your numbers so Roy doesn't get in trouble when he gets home."

Roy laughs good-naturedly and the people around him smile in his direction and join in the laughter.

I keep looking for my father but I can't see him and I don't want to give up my spot.

Fred starts talking. "Folks," he says, "you all know Charlie Kuehn. Charlie farmed his whole life right here on this place. Charlie has moved to the Good Shepherd Home for Retired People and sold the farm to the new owners, Mr. Arlan Kletzke and his daughter Ruth Joseph. Mr. Kletzke and Ms. Joseph plan to take over the reins from old Charlie and raise beef here."

Fred looks over the crowd until he spots me and then he finds my father somewhere in the back. "Would the new owners raise their arms so the good people here can see who you are?"

I feel embarrassed but I raise my arm and turn around to the crowd and smile. I feel like visiting royalty. People next to me move back a few inches, giving me some room.

"Now folks, you know retirement living doesn't come cheap and Charlie worked hard all his life and deserves a good retirement. So let's bid high on all these things"—he waves to the yard and wagons—"and give Charlie a good send off. First we'll do the small stuff on these two wagons, then we'll work around the yard, and then we'll finish back by the barn with the farm equipment. The last thing we'll sell is the truck and then we'll finish up with the guns and boat. And remember, when I say sold, it's yours. If you have any objections, speak up then."

One of the workers places a box of small items on a stool. The auctioneer reaches in and grabs a teapot. He holds it up. The worker reaches in and pulls out a small plate and a mug and holds them in the air for everyone to see.

Fred shifts his voice now, and begins to sing out, "Who'll start off the auction with a bid of one dollar. One dollar. One dollar for everything in this box."

The worker puts down what he has been holding and paws through the box and holds up two more items, a lacy doily, and an old picture frame."

"Folks," the auctioneer cries, "there's lots of good things in this box. We can't show you everything. That's why you had time to look it over before the auction started. Okay, now, will anyone bid a dollar? All right then, will anyone bid fifty cents, fifty cents for this nice box of stuff."

Suddenly one of the worker spots a hand raised in the crowd and indicates with a grunt to Fred that a bid has been made. Fred sings out, "I've got fifty cents, who'll bid a dollar? Yes, do I hear a dollar fifty. Yes, do I hear two? Two dollars I got. Do I hear three? Do I hear two dollars and fifty cents? Two dollars and fifty cents will take it. Do I hear three dollars? Sold for two dollars and fifty cents to number…."

Fred squints into the sunlight to make out the number and someone shouts from the crowd, "Number 58," and Fred says "Sold to number 58 for two dollars."

With the next box, when Fred can't get a dollar right away, he stops to tell us what he thinks we don't know.

"You know folks, all these things belonged to Charlie and Charlie's family. There are lots of old things in these boxes, antiques you can't find anywhere else. Don't be shy. You'll be sorry if you don't bring home some of these precious antiques. Who'll give me one dollar?" Fred scans the crowd and spots a hand and he's off and running.

The crowd around the wagons stays put. They watch intently, craning their necks to get a good look. The box of old china tempts me. It is delicate porcelain that seems to have grown more luminous with age, delicate pink roses painted in fine detail in a simple pattern. As the price climbs over one hundred dollars, I am beginning to lose my nerve, but then suddenly, Fred calls sold and looks at my number.

"Sold to number 33. I see them new folks know how to eat in style," he tells the crowd. "Maybe one of you men here will be one of the lucky fellows to get invited to eat at the table with Ruth. She's available you know. Of course, her father will be right there so you'll have to behave like a gentleman."

I try not to blush but I feel myself get red in the face at the same time that I am pleased that I am included in the teasing.

Finally Fred finishes with the boxes on the wagons and moves to the furniture. The crowd has thinned, but it is still hard to get close to the items being auctioned. Now the buyers look like they are from town. Young couples stand nervously while they bid against some of the antique dealers. The table and chairs come up and it looks like the set will sell for $150. My hand shoots up. I hear Fred call out my number after he shouts, "sold for $200".

My father appears then and we immediately move the chairs and table back into the dining room. Successful bidders have claimed little patches of lawn where they place items they have bought into piles. We drag the table back into the house. There is a closet in the dining room. We put the leaves in the box into the closet. I can see by the dust marks on the floor that this is where they have always been stored. I glance around the room, imagining how it will look when I put my collection of majolica platters up on the plate rails that line the walls, refinish the table, and put up pretty lace curtains and paint the room. One of the first things I will do, I decide, as I turn out the overhead light, is replace the light bulb with some of higher wattage. The fixture is beautiful though, copper and iron, in an ornate filigree design that resembles art Deco. I haul in the box of china and place it on the built-in oak buffet.

When we get back outside, the auction is mostly over and the crowd is starting to disperse. All that is left are the guns. Charlie had eight guns, and three bow and arrows and an old fishing boat. Bidding is hot and heavy amongst a handful of men. These men came for the guns and some plan to leave with them.

My father is still interested in watching the action so I meander back to the front yard. Most of the furniture has been hauled away. I look around to see what kind of perennial flowers grow here. When we had looked at the farm in January, the yard had been covered with snow.

I spot a row of peonies along side the road leading into the farm. I can see the deep burgundy tips of the plants pushing up. There is a large circular flowerbed off to one side. I study the dead foliage. It looks like a bed of day lilies, and maybe some irises as well. By the steps leading up to the porch, I see lily of the valley pips. I pick up cups, plates, and napkins that people have dropped on the lawn while I look. On Monday morning, the title is going to be signed over to us. I might as well start claiming ownership now. I go to the car for a bag to hold the garbage. Cars and trucks are pulling in, loading up their purchases. An old refrigerator sits forlornly on the side lawn. I don't imagine that the refrigerator sold, and it will have to be hauled off. A few kitchen chairs, metal with torn vinyl seats, are lying askew on the grass. Some of the cardboard boxes have been flung aside as well, bits of old newspaper blowing into the shrubbery.

Now that the auction is over, I want to find out what Fred thinks about how Charlie did so I can report back to Charlie. I track Fred down. He looks tired.

"Good, he did good," Fred says. "It was a good day for an auction. Folks have been waiting for this auction for some time. Charlie will be able to rest easy over in the home. I'll drive over and deliver the check to him personally. But you can call him, Ruth, and tell him what I said."

Then he is called away by a buyer who maintains that he bought an item for $50 less than what he was charged at the checkout table. Fred listens but doesn't give any ground. "I laid out the rules at the beginning of the auction," he says. "You got to pay attention to what I said. All bids are final. The clerk never makes a mistake," he adds. "Do you still want it?" he asks the man who is complaining. The man says that he guesses he does and goes off to pay.

The wind is picking up. A cold chill is descending. I want to get on the way. But my father is nowhere to be found, once more. I start searching. Behind the barn, my father is deep in conversation with a man who looks like a farmer. I approach them. Neither looks at me. I stood by their side, expecting my father to break away from the conversation and introduce me. He does not. I have figured out that my father is negotiating the purchase of a dozen beef heifers.

I blurt out, "Now wait a minute. I'm your partner and that means we make decisions together."

The men stopped talking. The farmer looks at me blankly. My father says nothing.

I try to soften my words. "Remember me? Your partner in crime?"

"Now Ruthie," my father says, starting to defend himself, "this man is offering us some good terms. I just thought…"

I interrupt. "I have to be included in all purchase decisions."

I was drawing a line in the sand. I was not, I was telling myself, going along for the ride. I wanted to be in the driver's seat next to my father. My father was doing exactly what my brother and sisters had warned me he would do when we had told them of our farm partnership.

"Dad will try to take over. He doesn't seem to know we're all adults with lives of our own, ideas of our own. He'll think you're a kid he can boss around," my brother had warned.

Before my father has time to respond to me, Fred comes rushing towards us. By his speed, I can tell he feels some urgency. The other man spots Fred and suddenly is in a hurry to get away.

"Well, work it out between the two of you. When you're ready to deal, give me a call." He walks away as Fred comes towards us.

"Howya doing George," Fred asks him as they pass. George ignores him. Fred joins us and stands to watch George. When he is out of earshot, Fred turns to us. "You have to be careful with that guy. He's a shyster. He'll try to sell you what you don't want cause it ain't no good."

Fred turns to me. "You got a good deal on that table, you know. That table was made by Charlie's grandfather. Same with the chairs. They'll never wear out. Say now," he says to both of us," I know a lot of people around here and I can give you good leads."

He looks back at George. "But stay away from that guy."

My father and I climb into the car. I know we have to talk about what happened. I know that he will not bring up the subject, that it will be up to me. But I know enough to know that we are both tired. It's been a long day. Our nerves are frayed. Now is not the time.

I steal a peak in the rear view mirror as we start down the long driveway. The cold still house seems so empty and forlorn that I can almost hear it crying, like a puppy taken from its mother too early, who needs a hot water bottle and ticking clock to reassure him that the world is safe. My father seems unaware of my mood. He starts telling me about some other leads on beef cattle, and prattles on the rest of the way home.

All I say in response is "I think we should give Fred a call. I think he's a good guy and we ought to get to know him better."

.

Chapter Four

Rain, Rain, Go Away

Thunder pierced the night. I awoke suddenly wide-awake. I stumbled to the window to watch lightning streak across the sky and strike land in the distance. The storm moved in.

I tried the lights but they had failed. I grabbed the flashlight I keep by my bed and crept downstairs so I wouldn't wake my father. But he had awakened as well and was sitting in an easy chair pulled to the front window so he could watch the storm.

"I see the storm woke you too Ruthie. Well, come join me then. It's a good one." He said, "Joe will be swearing. No way he'll be able to plow after a rain like this."

Joe was the custom operator who had done Charlie's farm work for him. We were going to have Joe do our fieldwork as well. I watched as sheets of water washed the house. Wind was wildly blowing the branches of the big trees. I felt the house shiver. I could hear the hunger of the wind, ferreting out small cracks in the windows, making eerie noises. The rain pulsated in the wind, banging against the side of the house like a hammer. I thought of all the storms this house had weathered and still it stood strong and tall.

My father and I sit in silence for some time. Then the storm began moving off to the east. Gradually the sound of the rain softened until the drops made pitter-pattering sounds on the roof and windows again. Now I felt like I could go back to bed. We had survived a big storm.

In the morning, I surveyed the land. At first I saw only small puddles and old furrows holding water. Then I discovered the lake in the southwest corner of the farm. The lake covered perhaps ten acres of land. Charlie had talked about that corner getting wet in the spring, but this seemed more like flooding to me. I called to my father to come upstairs. We looked at the small lake together.

"It'll take a while to dry out, and even then, the ground will be too saturated to work," my father told me. We regarded the sky with some uneasiness. It was leaden, gray, and the air felt heavy. When we turned on the television to catch the weather, we saw a large low-pressure system covering the western half of the United States, poised to move in our direction.

Day after day it rained. The lake now consumed most of the southwest forty. One evening I heard a raucous sound, and it took me awhile to sort out what the sound was. It was the honk of swans. When I went outside to look at the sky, I saw masses of them landing like small airplanes onto our lake. I could hardly believe what I was seeing. The water was now white with their feathers, so white that it almost looked like a big glacier floating on the field.

The rest of the fields were covered with big puddles hundreds of feet wide. Everywhere I looked I saw water. Inside, dampness made the house smell like a drawer of dirty socks, but the still, humid air brought no relief when I opened windows.

When I touched the kitchen cabinets, they were sticky with old varnish and oil from fingers and food touching them for years. I drew buckets of hot water and added oil soap and scrubbed until they felt better. But there was nothing I could do about the fields. I looked out the windows glumly as more rains fell.

One day I was seized with a desire to see the swans up close. I put on rubber barn boots and started picking my way out to the lake. When I took a step in the mud, I struggled to pull the boots back with my foot remaining inside. The mud sucked me down into its soup. My clothes were wet from my sweat.

I almost turned back half a dozen times. At one point, I couldn't get my foot back from the mud. The effort of pulling on my leg threw me off balance. Before I could stop myself, I fell forward into mud. I put out my hands to stop myself from falling headfirst and landed in a gigantic puddle. I struggled back up. Now I was covered in mud, from my hands to my knees. My clothes clung.

I searched for an easier way. I decided to follow the road between the fields. There, I could pick my way through high and low spots. The earth packed down by years of tractor traffic held the water on the surface in large pools. I splashed water up, but at least I didn't sink into mud.

When I got closer, I pulled the binoculars out of my pocket and looked at the swans. I could see the swans so clearly that the black markings near their bright yellow beaks were sharp and distinct. I made out their individual feathers. I was struck by their beauty and grace. They swam around as if this were really a lake, mucking in the water with their beaks. I wiped some of the mud off my hands before I took out the camera I remembered to bring along. I wanted photos to show Charlie.

Then I started the struggle back to the farmhouse. I fell several more times but I no longer cared how muddy I became. My boots were so heavy from mud caked to the bottom that they impeded my progress. I tried to stamp it off, but I only succeeded in picking up more. I continued down the road, winding past the fields and finally I reached the house. I climbed the back steps and kicked off the boots, removed my jacket. My pants were too dirty to wear into the house. I opened the back door and called for my father.

"Ruthie, what the heck happened to you?" he asked, when he came to the door.

"Bring me an old towel, anything so I can get out of these pants," I answered. Suddenly I felt weary, exhausted, and discouraged. Is this an omen how life on the farm would go?

When he returned, I wrapped the towel around me and took off my jeans. I left the mess on the steps and went inside.

My father gives a low whistle. "That's not a field, that's a swamp."

I agreed and headed upstairs to wash off the mud.

When I returned, he was sitting at the kitchen table. "This looks pretty bad, Ruthie. Pretty bad."

"I know," I answer. Between us is silence so palpable I could touch it. I am blaming him for the mess we are in. But I don't want to say it aloud. A part of me also knows he isn't really to blame. I am telling myself that I should never have said I would do this. We are both crazy. We retreat to separate rooms to brood alone.

The next day, Charlie calls. He wants to see the swans. I borrow the truck to drive over to his apartment to bring him back. Our driveway has become too muddy for my small car to navigate. We look from the yard at the patch of white in the distance.

"Haven't seen this is thirty years," Charlie says. "Ain't they beautiful? My mother always called the lake 'Lake Sally.'"

"You mean it's been here before?" I am astonished by that piece of information. "Is that what you meant when you said that corner gets real wet in the spring?"

"I had in mind a big puddle, not a lake. This is not how it usually gets, but this is an unusual year. If you're lucky, you'll only see this once. That's what makes it so memorable. When I was a young man, my mother named the lake after a great aunt who made it out for a visit every ten years or so. Mark this down on a calendar somewhere. You'll want to remember it in a drought year."

"Oh I think I'll remember the year. We're going to call the lake Lake Charlie in your honor," I joke. "Charlie's Lake with the thousand swans."

Charlie's blue eyes twinkle with glee. "A sense of humor is a good thing. If you're going to farm, you need to have a sense of humor. Because there's not a darn thing you can do about it except laugh. You know I can't remember what I ate for lunch, but I can remember back over all the years I farmed and can come pretty close to the year different things happened. You'd think all the farming would blur together. But each year is different. Each year the weather acts a certain way, different from the last, different from the next. I can't think of one year that was the same as another."

I merely nod, thinking of how differently an outsider would view farming life. Three months ago I'd have thought it was pretty much all the same.

But it is hard to laugh when it rains everyday for the next two weeks. It rained all day; it rained all night. I thought I was going to lose my mind. My father and I snapped at each other over trivial things. We stayed in opposite corners of the house.

One morning sun shone through the clouds. The sky started to clear. Wind started blowing from the west. The old windows whistled and shrieked. The sound was reedy, like a blues tune played by a badly tuned clarinet. My father said the wind was a good thing. Together wind and sun would dry out the land.

I kept my eyes on Lake Charlie. Each day the edges receded. One day when I had driven into the big city to buy groceries, the swans departed. I wished I had been there when they'd taken off. I could imagine the sight as the wings of the birds beat together, rising in mass to head towards their final destination somewhere up north.

My father said the sound was like nothing he had ever heard. He had gone to the window and watched. The birds rose almost in unison from the lake, beating their wings, rising up in a cloud, like smoke from a fire, crying loudly, forming into a long loose group, then flying higher into a tighter group, and then finally swans had flown ahead of the mass until a "V" hung there in the sky for a moment, then pointed north, and then silence.

Both of us watched the calendar. April was done. Fieldwork needed to be underway. Oats planted first as a cover for hay or alfalfa, then corn, then soybeans, but my father said he wasn't worried. He said it was a mistake to plant too soon, before the ground had warmed. Seeds need warmth and sun to sprout.

It wasn't only our land that was lying untouched. The neighbors hadn't been able to get into their fields either.

Weather seemed to improve in May. The beginning of the month was dry. On May 10, the sound and sight of tractors working all around our farm quickened my hopes. But optimism was tempered by reality. I could see moisture in the furrows, the pond fading but still there. All around me I smelled the funky dank smell of waterlogged ground.

At supper, my father was quiet. "I have never seen anything like this in all my years as a seed salesman. We've got to get our fieldwork started. Oats won't germinate if it gets too warm. For every day forward from today, we'll be losing corn production. We need those crops or it won't be profitable to feed cattle. We're lucky we don't have cattle to feed right now. The price of hay will go up, so will corn and soybeans if this weather continues."

"Maybe we've seen the worst," I say.

"Look out to the west. There are storm clouds coming our way. Some of our neighbors have sandy soil. Maybe they'll get their crops in. But we need more dry weather, maybe two weeks worth. No, it doesn't look like we're going to get the kind of weather we need."

"We never should have bought this farm," I blurt out, no longer able to keep those thoughts to myself.

My father remains unruffled. He shrugs off my remark. "No, things could be worse. Be patient, Ruthie. This isn't the way things will be. We can't snap our fingers at Mother Nature and expect that she will give us the kind of weather we want. We have to wait it out. When the time is right, we'll act."

I bite my tongue and do not respond with my real thoughts. I am thinking that it is easy for him to say. He's been around farmers all his life. I am glad we don't know anybody around here. The neighbors must be laughing at us, two fools who thought they could waltz in, buy up a farm, and start farming when we didn't know any more about farming than the man in the moon. I wanted to say that to my father but I knew he would only lecture me on patience. I had spent the last ten years listening to my husband tell me I had to learn to act not react. Now my father was telling me I had to do just the opposite.

One night after dark, I was cleaning up the kitchen when I heard a truck driving down the gravel driveway. We don't get many visitors. I peered out at a shining red pick-up, fancy with accessories, rumbling as the diesel engine idled. I went to the door. Under the light at the back door I could see a tall, good-looking man. He looked tired.

I opened the door. "Joe Hansen," he said, stretching out his hand, "and you must be Ruthie." Only my father called me by my pet name. I wasn't sure I liked it coming out of a stranger's mouth, but let it go. "Is your father around?"

I went after my father, working on the house wiring down the basement.

"What are we going to do, Arlan? Ground is too wet to work, even with the quad trac?" Joe asked my father.

My father tilted his head in my direction. "Ruth and I are partners. We never make decisions without first talking it over between us."

I gave a slight smile and looked at them both. My father and I had been arguing endlessly these last weeks over his wanting to make decisions alone. He did not want to concede his authority because, as he liked to point out, I didn't know the first thing about farming. And I argued that if we were really partners, we would decide together. I held my ground even though he was stubbornly against it. I made the point over and over that I would never learn unless I was involved. His stubbornness made me want to learn even more. I responded with my own stubbornness. In the end, I knew I hadn't changed his mind so much as worn him down. He had finally pleaded for peace.

"Ruth, if you and I continue on like we are, we are going to be enemies. I don't want to be alienated from my own daughter. Let's agree to work together with some harmony, for the sake of happiness. I grant you that I am an old man who's not used to sharing decisions with a woman, and you grant me that I am willing to change. Let's make the best of a bad situation."

We had shaken on our truce. I knew that he was trying to live up to his part of the bargain.

Joe, and my father and I sat in the kitchen and tossed around the facts and the alternatives. We went over an essentially unsolvable situation until we were sick and tired of talking about it. We finally decided we couldn't work ground that couldn't be worked. And due to the lateness of the season, maybe we wouldn't be able to plant anything at all. We'd have to wait and see.

Now that we had worked that out between the three of us, I offered Joe some pie.

I bustled around the kitchen, pulling out a lemon meringue pie the two of us have been working on. I cut Joe a big piece and set it in front of him with a glass of milk. Being included in the discussion had cheered me. We start talking about things in general.

"This will hurt me too. I've only put in half the acres I normally put in. I've got to pay on that equipment whether I get a crop or not. Good thing my wife is a teacher. At least, we'll eat. Her salary can't cover all my expenses but it'll keep a roof over our heads and buy food," Joe said. "Wish I'd known about this before I bought that new pick-up," he added, gesturing towards the driveway. The pick-up was still rumbling in the chilly night air.

After another long discussion, we concluded that we still had a few more weeks to plant corn, although we'd have to shorten up the variety and take a hit in yield. We all seemed more optimistic, buoyed up by the other's hopes for better weather.

"If we haven't got you planted by the first week of June, I don't know what you'll do," Joe said, "but we'll leave it hanging for now."

Every day we checked the soil for moisture. Even as late as the second week of June, the soil stayed in a tight ball when we held it in our hand. By now the season was so advanced that corn would no longer mature by frost. Time has long since passed to plant oats.

So we decided to plant winter rye on the fields in late summer, then plow that into the ground next spring. Rye would improve the fertility and help hold back the weed crop. We'd try to hay the fields planted in clover. We agreed to hold off on buying livestock. Next spring we'd get the farm into full operation.

I'd decided that I needed some type of job. Staying home on the farm without farm chores to occupy me had given me too much free time. I was not used to not working. I needed to start meeting other people. I needed more social contacts than my father. I had painted and cleaned and moved the furniture around a dozen times. I was bored. My father was bored. In between rains, he weeded the garden and repaired the house. We had run out of topics of conversation.

I took the first job I could find in Rush River, hardly a hotbed of employment opportunities, working as a teller in the local credit union. The pay was bad, but I would meet people. My father reminded me that low pay is better than no pay. I did not want to drive to Clear Water every day nor did I want to take the type of work I was qualified for. As discouraged as I felt, I was not yet ready to go back to the way I had been living. Maybe I was learning a modicum of patience.

The wild flowers growing in the ditch made me recall the first year after I had moved out West. Death Valley had enough rain for a hundred year flood. My husband and I took a trip through the dry arid valley after the rains ended. For miles, we saw a sea of colors. Yellows, purples, pink, usually in masses because the seeds requiring certain conditions were clustered together. The flowers had been breathtakingly beautiful. Even the boundaries of the wash waters, their dry beds turned to flowers once water had disappeared, were visible.

The farm ditches everywhere in the township bloomed just as Death Valley had that year. The difference was the amount of rain. In Death Valley, less than five inches of rain produced the breath-taking panorama. We'd had 20 inches in June and nearly 30 inches in the month of July. The rains executed the only redeeming aspect of the summer.

Hoary alyssum, common tansy, black-eyed Susan, butter and eggs, pickerelweed, Joe–pye, sunflowers, Indian pipe, asters, daisies, flowers in profusion making my daily walk a joy. I picked bouquets of flowers and arranged them, dragging out every vase I could find. Pickle jars, glass pitchers, water glasses were called to new duty. Every day I walked and picked an arm full of blooms, and arranged them on every tabletop in the house. Our house looked like a florist's shop. Too late, I realize that I should have taken photographs to preserve the memory of the year the earth bloomed flowers instead of corn and soybeans.

Charlie tried to reassure us both. "Next year will be different," he'd say. "If you just wait, the weather will change."

Chapter Five
Haying

The clover field in the middle eighty acres passed its prime several weeks ago. My father has been fretting about this, bringing in a clump of the dark green aromatic clover every few days. Now purple blossoms color the field, casting a haze over the dark green stems and leaves. I knew better than to call the field beautiful out loud but I secretly thought the fully headed field of clover was a beautiful sight, especially on a rare day with sun. The field smells as sweet and clean as spring rain, attracting honeybees that buzz around busily harvesting nectar. Their hives will be full of sweet clover honey.

My father has found a farmer up the road from us, a Mennonite, who wants to make hay to feed his dry cows. We have had a temporary clearing in the weather, and my father tells me as I eat breakfast before work, that today is the day haying will begin.

The Mennonite farmer does not plan to make hay into bales, but instead is planning to cut and chop the clover for haylage. The clover is so thick that it will never dry down unless we have several days of hot dry weather. Fewer and fewer farmers put up small bales anymore even though most people think of that when they think of hay.

Haylage can be chopped and laid into a bunker silo instead of being blown into an upright silo. The haylage is covered with plastic to prevent spoilage from exposure to air, and old tires are put on top of the plastic to seal the bunker. To feed, the farmer moves the tires away, peels back the plastic tarp and uses a skid steer to scoop out haylage. This means less work and no worry about silo unloaders breaking down at feeding time, especially in the dead of winter when machinery complains about cold weather. It's a practical method.

To prepare, my father has been hauling old tires that Charlie had tucked away back in the woods with the oaks, maples and walnuts.

We had checked out the woods one Sunday and discovered that the history of the farm's machinery was scattered under the trees, along with every tire that had ever worn out. It was a shock to come upon the discards without any forewarning. The machinery had been parked in neat rows, as if waiting for the farmer to return to hitch a piece to his tractor. There were three long rows, about fifty feet in length, under the trees canopies. If I had been a child, I would have run to the old rusty machinery with joy, and played games, pretending to drive or ride the equipment, some of which had iron seats to sit upon.

Charlie had been neat and orderly about everything else, but the woods was so thick with old machinery that it took beauty away from the hardwoods. I know it bothered my father. He is the neatest, tidiest person I have ever known. He would mutter under his breath the days he was moving the tires. It was hard work. Grass and shrubs had grown up around and between and through them, but if he pulled, and tugged, and dragged hard enough he could get the tires free. We now had a stack of 50 old tires behind the barn where he is storing them until he could load them into his truck to take over to the other farm. The Mennonite said he is glad to have them. Storing haylage this way was something he was trying for the first time.

My father had cleared the ground of grass and shrubs where he was storing the tires. Next year he plans to break the ground for more garden space. Vine crops that have been known to take over the garden while you sleep will go there and the sweet corn. This year's crop of sweet corn has been blown sideways twice by winds, and twice my father has gone up and down the rows righting the stocks, burying the roots deeper, propping up the corn until it can stand on its own. The down draft from wind seems to be just right in that spot and nowhere else.

He has another pile started back behind the barn, this for scrap metal from the old machinery. He will haul this off to the salvage yard to sell. He's bought a used tractor to help him in the clean up.

I am ready to leave for work. I am sorry that I am going to miss the first real farming this farm has seen since we took ownership.

When I pulled up to the farm that evening, the house looked deserted. I could hear the sound of motors working and make out on the horizon farm equipment, but it looked like nothing was happening. The chopper had made only a few swaths in the field of clover. I changed my clothes and hiked down the road to get a closer look.

As I approached, I could see what had happened. The tractor pulling the chopper had gotten stuck in one of the wet holes in the hay field. The lush clover had made it hard to see wet spots. The clover was so overgrown that by now it was a tangle of long stems, flowering heads, and heads that had gone to seed. There was one tractor pulling on one side, and another tractor pulling from the other side. My father was on one of the tractors.

I watched the wheels spin on his tractor. Evidently now there were two tractors stuck in the mud. The man on the other tractor jumped down and walked towards my father. They conferred over the back wheels of the tractor, then the man disconnected the chain he was using to pull out the tractor pulling the chopper, and hopped back onto his tractor and drove around until he was well away from the tractor my father was on. He jumped down and hooked up the chain to that tractor. Then my father disconnected his chain to the chopper and tractor, and climbed back on.

The big tractor sputtered and puffed, but the wheels dug in the field and my father took off freed from the mud. They repositioned the tractors around the stuck equipment, and when the farmer gave the sign, they both started pulling. I could see the chopper and tractor budge just a little. Then they spotted me.

My father shouted something and both tractors shut down. My father gestured to me to come. When I got there, he waved me over to the stuck equipment. It seems I was to hop on, and when it started moving, I was to push down the clutch, throw it into gear, and take off towards higher ground away from the mud hole. My father showed me what to do. I nodded that I understood, and both men left me and climbed back on their tractors.

My hands were shaking I was so nervous. I wanted to do it right, but I had never even been on a tractor before. There was no time for me to think about that, or study the tractor. I sat there poised to throw the tractor into gear. They revved their engines, started pulling, and I could feel the wheels on my tractor roll forward. I pushed down the clutch, threw it into gear, depressed the gas, and let up on the clutch, as I started moving forward. As the wheels left the mud, my tractor picked up speed. I was moving easily now.

My father shouted, "Stop, Ruthie" but it took a minute for his order to register. I pulled my foot off the gas, and lurched forward over the steering wheel. I turned around and looked back. We had moved fifty feet and were clear of the mud hole. My father gave me thumbs up. I jumped down from the tractor, falling into the field of clover, and took a victory roll. When my body crushed the leaves, more aromas floated up. It smelled good enough to eat.

My father and the other man came towards me. This was Howard, the Mennonite who was buying the hay. When we talked, I found myself staring at his teeth, as smooth and white and perfect as any I had ever seen. Howard was telling us that it was getting so late he didn't think he'd cut any more clover today. "I'll be back tomorrow," he promised. Because of the problems in the field, he had three tractors on our farm. He wanted my father to drive one back; he'd drive the other. I was to drive over in the car and pick up my Dad.

On our way back to the house, my father slumped a little in his seat. "Farming is more work than I expected, Ruthie," he admitted to me. "I wish your mother could have seen you today, driving that tractor out of the mud hole. You look like you've farmed all your life."

"Is that so?" I replied. I would never admit my fear to my father. He was starting to show that he respected me, and I wasn't going to say anything that would make him change his mind.

I went to the calendar in the kitchen where I had been noting significant events. I wrote, "haying begins."

Chapter Six
Buying Beef Cows

Arlan is pointing to a picture of a beef cow, going over the finer qualities of what constitutes a good one. He has moved to a new topic, having exhausted the differences between breeds. I have listened to him for months weighing the merits of Hereford compared to Black Angus. The white-faced beef cow with red hair was a gentle animal with a good disposition. We had decided on Herefords.

Fred had told us about two batches of beef cattle that might be for sale. We were going to see an old couple who would be holding an auction to liquidate their dairy operation in the spring. In addition to their dairy herd, they had two dozen Hereford heifers for sale that they were willing to sell before the auction.

Fred spoke highly of the couple and the cows they kept, praising their genetics and their health. He'd also made a point of mentioning that if they sold us the heifers, his commission would be less at the auction. "But I always like to help a neighbor," Fred had told us, and I was beginning to believe him. We had picked up another small tractor to clear snow from the driveway following Fred's leads.

So one January day we set out to visit the farm. While we were there, I hoped to get a tour of the dairy barn as well. We took the back roads, passing farm after farm. I studied each one, noticing the arrangement of the buildings, what the houses looked like, trying to imagine who lived there. We saw many barns with their lights on. Work was being done.

When we drove in, my first impression was how run down the farm looked. The house needed a siding job, or at least repainting. The sheds were gray, leaning to one side or the other. The old barn looked pretty sorry as well, hardly any red paint left on the old barn boards. We banged on the door of the house, and an old man appeared. He motioned for us to come inside.

The house was warm and comfy. He and his wife were finishing up their dinner, the plates pushed back to make room for a piece of pie. Everything was clean and shiny inside, the smell of wood smoke in the air, along with a whiff of fresh coffee. We sat down across from them. They offered us some homemade pie. Fat red cherries were spilling out from the crust, oozing juice. We accepted the offer.

They explained that they were retiring after a lifetime of milking cows. They planned to have an auction in March, selling all the equipment and cows. Then, the wife informed me, they were going to fix up the old place and take a Florida vacation in the winter.

We headed down to the barn. When we stepped inside the barn, I heard the lowing of the cows. The feeling was comforting, like the stable where Jesus was born. Most of the cows were lying down. The old farmer moved slowly, so we did too. The cows looked in our direction, but stayed down, resting and relaxed. Despite the shabby appearance of the barn, the inside was very much in order and clean. By the door where we entered, two scrapers stood at the ready. A feed cart was pushed up into a corner. The barn desk was neatly organized.

The center aisle that led down between the two rows of stanchions glistened white from the lime that had been put down by a spreader. I could see neat piles of feed in front of the cows. The cows were lying on black rubber mattresses with some straw bedding underneath. The gutters were clean, though there were growing patches of manure behind the cows. Country music was floating out from somewhere. This felt like a home, a cow home, I thought. These are lucky cows, I also found myself thinking. Off in a corner, I could see a pen with some babies in it. As my eyes adjusted to the darkness, I could make out what a Jersey looked like.

"The beef cows are out back in a loafing shed," the old man explained.

"Could we look around here a bit?" I asked.

"Sure, no problem," he answered. "You like cows, do you?" he asked me.

I just smiled. We started down the center aisle. As we passed, the cows started getting up. I could see that Jerseys are small. Some of them turned around to gaze at us. Curious creatures. The colors were brown but most had patches of white mixed in, like cream floating on top of a cup of hot coffee before it mixed in.   Their feet were dainty, pointed, like Cinderella's glass slippers. The tails were switching back and forth. I looked at one of the cows that had turned her head to look at me, gazing into a cow face.

The big brown eyes were liquid, the color of gingerbread. I had never seen a prettier face. This one had a topknot of straw colored hair. Her muzzle was tan, with freckles.   I wanted to reach right over and put a bow in her hair. The old man could tell I wanted to see them from the front, so he pointed out the feed alley in front of the cow. But first he wanted me to slip on some plastic booties over my shoes. "You wouldn't want anyone walking on your plate, would you?", the old guy asked.

My father walked down the center aisle. As he passed, the cows stood up, dropping a pile of manure, and turned around to gaze at him. "What time you milk last?" he asked.

"Six straight up. Milk truck comes at 7:30 AM, every day, second stop on the route."

I came back around and followed by father down the aisle. These cows were built. They were almost as wide as they were long, with big udders. I could see they had quite a store of milk in them already. When we got down to one end, I noticed those udders were flat and flabby. " I've got a dozen dry cows," the old farmer said. I dried them up two weeks ago.

"Do you use a bull?" my father asked.

"Never have. Jerseys are easy to breed. My wife spends some time down in the cow yard when I let them out after lunch. She does a good job detecting heats. I usually give them some hay out in the lot, clean out the feed alleys, and bring them in for evening milking. We take good care of our cows. They're good to us so we're good to them."

"You want to help me let them out?" the old farmer asked me.

"Sure," I answered. "What do I do?"

The old farmer looked at my Dad.

My Dad could tell what he was wondering. "Ruthie doesn't know much about cows but she'll learn." That drew laughter from the old man.

I walked down the feed alley opening up the stanchions. Some of the cows pulled back hard. I could tell they were anxious to get outside. He had told me to stop at the dry cows.

"We let them out later," he explained. "They don't need such good hay. They clean up after the milking herd."

I stood in the barn lot and watched the cows. Some of them came up to me, sniffing me. I petted them. They seemed to like it. I noticed none of these cows had numbers in their ears. I asked the old farmer about that.

"Oh, we know all their names. So do they."

"Really?" I thought he was kidding.

"Watch me," he said, "You let out one of them dry cows."

I watched as he called out "Susie, Susie, Hey bossy."

A dark brown cow with great white patches on her flanks separated from the herd and came our way. The old farmer shoed her into the barn. "Ho, Bossy, into your stanchion," he said. He followed Susie down the aisle and I watched as she entered way down at the end, next to her sisters. I was amazed.

"Come over here and look at the calves," the old farmer suggested. I followed him to the back corner. There were two pens back there, full of clean straw and hanging from the front of the pens, two buckets with nipples on the side. "We don't have any of them fancy calf hutches, but we have good luck with our calves. Haven't had one die in quite some time. These are about four weeks old and starting to get the hang of drinking from a nipple bucket. Cute little babies, aren't they?"

The calves had as much sway on me as kittens have on children. They looked gangly on long thin legs with big brown eyes. They started to kick up their heels and run around the pen just like wild horses.

"Feeling their oats, aren't they?" the farmer commented. "Well, you ready to look at the cattle?" I left reluctantly.

The beef calves weren't nearly as cute as the Jerseys. We looked them over carefully, as much as we could with the herd of them roiling around in the open shed fenced off from the dairy cows. Herefords are meaty looking animals with curly red hair, not placid like dairy cows, more on the frisky side. I liked their white faces and red lips. Their coats were thick from staying out in the cold all winter, their red hair curly. The shed had piles of straw but not as fresh as the dairy cows. A metal bale feeder had a big round bale in it that had been half eaten.

"All my hay was good this year. I had it trucked in from South Dakota after our wet summer when it was impossible to make good hay. I made that into silage. These cows have eaten like royalty all winter, and it's cost me a fortune. But they are good and healthy."

My father pulled me off to the side to confer with me on buying them. We both agreed, which was a welcomed change from our usual wrangling over what was the best decision. "Let me bargain a little," my father begged.

I told him to give it a try. He negotiated with the farmer and got him to drop his price $50 a head if we took them home before the week was out because he'd be saving on feed costs.

On our way out, we stopped in the milk house and he showed me around. The room was sparkling clean. A stainless steel tank sat in the middle of the room. He called it the bulk tank. Milk would flow from the milking units through the pipeline into the tank where it would be cooled down to the right temperature. A double sink sat in front of a sunny window. Over one sink hung milking units that were attached to the automatic washing system. A hot water tank sat in the corner, and next to that was a hand sink. In the other corner was a cupboard. He opened it to show me the collection of items: milk filters, parts for the milking units in case one of them failed, a pen, and a drinking glass.

"This is the best water down here in the milk house", he said, as he filled a glass and took a big drink. "Sweet and cold, just like the milk."

Off in another corner were two large containers. Detergent and solvents for the pipeline he told me. Outside the window, I could see remnants of last year's flowers. "The tulips will be coming up soon," he offered. "Ma always looks forward to that day."

We headed up to the house. The old lady motioned for me to come into the living room. She pointed to a chair, and then sat down in the one across from it. She reached down into a basket and pulled out some knitting. "Do you knit?" she inquired brightly.

"No, but I'd like to learn," I said, which was partially true. My mother had knitted beautiful sweaters and scarves and had taught me the basic stitches. I hadn't knitted in years though, so I wasn't sure I could remember how. The old lady showed me her sweater, a beautiful soft pink fuzzy jacket she was making for her granddaughter. Then she started to knit in earnest and we began to talk.

"Are you helping your father, or do you work out?" she started out the conversation. I filled her in on the history of our farming project.

She listened attentively. "Well, I knew nothing of farming when I married Albert. I was from the city. I liked Albert because he had such good manners and was so patient. He had a good sense of humor too, and good common sense. I started coming out on the farm to visit him after we started seeing each other and it sort of grew on me. When he asked me to marry him, I didn't hesitate."

"We've had a good life together. We raised our four children to be good people and they all helped in turn on the farm. We were never rich, but we always had food to eat, and lots of laughter. It is a good life, but you never get rich and you have to work all the time. But there are worse things you could do with your life. I think the part I enjoyed most was being my husband's partner. We worked together, side by side. He was there to help with the children, and I was there to help with the farm. We got to know each other's good and bad points very intimately. And we always had a laugh, no matter what went wrong. I can't complain about too much. You think the cows are pretty?" she asked with great earnestness.

"Yes, I do," I replied sincerely, half expecting her to laugh.

"Well, then, Ruth, I think you'll be a good farmer."

"Why?" I asked.

"Because if you think they're pretty, then you will learn to love them. If you love the cows, then you won't mind taking care of them. You'll be interested in everything that happens to them and that will make you a good farmer."

Chapter Seven

A Father's Dream, A Daughter's Dream

Things are changing with my father, my picture of him, and just as I seem to have a clearer picture, he changes again.

When we order seed for the coming crop year, he has become the customer while someone else fills his old role. Wayne, our seed salesman, sits at the kitchen table, laptop computer open and begins filling in the order.

My father eyes the computer uneasily. "I never had to use one of them things. Does that work pretty good for you?"

Wayne looks up. "Saves a lot of time. And, I can tell you immediately if I have the variety and day length of corn you want. I don't have to go back and refigure orders like I used to. Tallies up the total too; figures in the discount." My father peers over Wayne's shoulder, looking dubious.

"Well, that's good to know," he says. He goes on to a topic where he is more comfortable. "I've been telling Ruthie that a good salesman can look at an ear of corn and tell you the variety. Isn't that right Wayne?"

Wayne looks up from the computer again. "It used to be that way but now there are so many varieties of corn, it is hard to do. I heard that about you, though, Arlan. All the farmers around here would scratch their heads in wonderment. How did you do it?"

"I could tell by how long the ear was, how many rows in the ear. Even the color of the corn silk sometimes helped. I could remember what they planted but I never told them that. I liked to leave them wondering how I could look at the ear and tell them the variety. It really impressed them, made it easier for me to come back and get their order the next year. Besides, there weren't that many varieties, and all the farmers had their own favorites."

I wiggled in my chair. We were at the kitchen table. Most farm business is conducted at the kitchen table. I picked up one of the glossy sales brochures describing the different hybrids. I looked at the chart that showed the corn characteristics they used in their ratings. "Which one of these is most important?" I asked, turning to Wayne first for the answer, but trying to include my father as well. "It seems like thirty-six is an overwhelming number."

My father reached out with his pen. "Well it is Ruthie, but some are more important that the others. I think some of those are just hype, makes it look like the seed companies invented corn. I don't know what the Indians would say about that."

He started checking off on the chart. He selected five characteristics. "These cover the important points, don't you think Wayne?"

Wayne studied the check marks for a minute. "I think you've pretty much got it covered. I might consider adding stock strength. The wind can really blow here in the valley."

I try to imagine how my father acted when he was helping his customers. Wayne is patient, letting us mull over our decisions, helping us find the right mix of varieties to order. He tells a joke now and then to ease the tension. I could imagine my father acting the same way. Buying seed is a large expenditure. We are putting a lot of money on the line.

My father goes on to explain that corn is rated by characteristics. Each rating is one aspect of growing a strong corn plant that yields high, dries down fast, withstands heavy winds and rain, tolerates drought, produces a heavy full ear, resists disease and pests, and reacts well to herbicides. All this data helps in the selection of the best variety for our soil and how we will use the corn.

As we study the seed catalog, we are trying to guess at the growing season to come. Will it be an early spring? A wet spring? Will frost come early or on schedule?

We bet, and hedge the bets, buying different varieties, hoping weather matches selections. We'll buy some for the grain, and some to make corn silage for the cattle.

It's a long afternoon at the table. I am glad when Wayne finally prints out the order, leaving us a copy. He loads up his computer and printer. "Just a minute," he says with a grin, "I've got something for you". He winks at my father. When he comes back from his truck, he is carrying two Pioneer Seed caps. "I usually leave just one, but I think Ruth needs her own cap, don't you Arlan?"

My father is happy to have a new cap. I put mine on and go look in a mirror to see how it looks. Wayne and my father seem to enjoy that touch of feminine vanity. Wayne leaves me a new knife, a small paring knife to cut off sweet corn. "I only give these out to my extra special customers," he says, winking at me one more time before he takes off for his next appointment.

"Whew, that was a lot of work," my father says after Wayne is gone. "I'm glad I retired when I did. I wouldn't want to have to use a computer and jockey all that stuff around in my pea-sized brain. I know one thing for sure, I need a nap."

One Sunday my father and I were eating a lazy breakfast. Morning chores were out of the way. We had nothing to do until evening. My father was feeling mellow. Some of the discord between us had subsided. We had made some strategic decisions together. We had bought cattle. We had bought seed. We had created a business plan, using my expertise with the computer to analyze various cash flow scenarios. I think we were beginning to realize that each of us had something to offer. He knew more about agronomy and cattle. I had business expertise and knew how to plug numbers into spreadsheets. I had been trained to pay attention to the bottom line. Maybe our partnership would work after all.

My father pushed his plate away, put his elbows on the table. I knew this meant he was going to talk.

He began, "I had four dreams as a young man. If I fulfilled them, I figured I'd lived life the way I wanted. First of all, I wanted to read the Bible from beginning to end. I did that when I served in the Army, I started reading on page one and read all the way to the end. Then I started over. I hadn't met your mother yet."

I nodded to let him know I was listening.

He continued, "When I met your mother, I wanted to marry her right from the start. I knew that she was better than I was and would make me better. A man needs a good woman more than a woman needs a good man. That's the way men are. They need their women."

"I'll remember that you told me that," I joked with him.

"I always wanted to go to South America. When I was a kid, I used to dream of hitchhiking to the coast, and finding a boat that would take me there. Little did I know that by selling seed corn, I would fulfill that dream. When Jacques Seed started buying some of their seed corn from companies down there, I got the opportunity to live out that dream. When I won the trip to Brazil, it was exciting to finally get to see a piece of that continent. Too bad I was old when I went. It was too hot for me, and I didn't enjoy the trip nearly as much as I enjoyed dreaming about it."

I fingered the belt he had brought back from the trip. I listened with interest to what he had to tell me. "I always dreamed of owning a farm. I should have bought one right away when I was a young man starting out my life. But by the time I met your mother, it seemed like the time for doing that had passed. She didn't want to live on a farm. She liked the city, and never shared my love for country life. I used to bring it up ever so often, but she'd tell me how hard it would be to make a living, especially with four children to support. I suppose she was right, but I always regretted not trying harder to make that dream happen."

"When you get to the end of your life, regret is a big word to use. It implies that your whole life is a mistake. I'm not saying that. I loved your mother. We had a good marriage. I love you children. But I went along, avoided risks, and played it too safe. I was a good seed salesman, and the company never saw my real worth. I would have been a better father, a better husband, if I had made different choices. Sometimes you can't undo what you unintentionally taught."

I was starting to feel uncomfortable; getting the drift that my father felt in some way that he had been a failure. I certainly didn't think so but when I tried to interrupt him, he waved me aside. "Let me get to my point, Ruthie. Then I'll let you talk."

He continued, "When you said yes to buying the farm, you took the risk I was always afraid of taking. Now I'm an old man, set in my ways, and yet I've learned from you. Your courage gave me courage. If I had done this earlier, the course of my life would have flowed in a different direction. Being an authentic person is the hardest thing any of us has to do. I'm afraid I didn't do a very good job."

"You're doing it now" I interrupted. "You're even finding out you're not so set in your ways. It wasn't more than a few months ago when we were fighting like cats and dogs because you wanted to make all the decisions yourself. Besides, I don't think of myself as courageous. It's more like I don't know what I really want out of life. I certainly don't think of you as a failure."

My father seemed not to hear. "Some things can't be undone," he answered. "Every parent hopes their children will do what they did not do. The world needs people who live with integrity and courage, who think for themselves. I didn't figure out until recently that I couldn't get my kids to do that unless I did it first. I know you bought this farm because I wanted you to."

"No, I wanted that too," I interrupted.

He smiled patiently at me. I knew he was right. I wouldn't have wanted any of this without his wanting me to want it.

My father started talking again. "Yes, I know you wanted to but maybe not for the reasons that I'm talking about. I'm talking about when you feel a fire in your belly, a need to do something that you can't push aside, can't ignore. You'll be a good farmer. And maybe the taste of land in your mouth will be like the taste of sugar, sweet and addicting. But I don't think this is all there is for you, Ruthie. You're just beginning to discover your passions. You've taken the first step. You've started living your life on your own terms. But it's like going on a great and long exploration. You aren't quite sure what you expect to find, but you'll know it when you've found it. You're still young. I don't think this is the end for you. But it's a good place for you to start."

Again I tried to interrupt. But he kept talking. "Maybe this isn't the end for me either. All I know is that I couldn't stop wanting this until I got it. Now I'll do the best I can with the time I have left. When I'm gone, and God willing, that isn't going to happen soon, I don't see you doing this alone. Maybe you'll stay on the farm. The land calls to you. I see that. But maybe some day you won't be here. You don't know what will happen as you change. I can't make a permanent claim on you. You have to lead your own life. You're going to find someone you love and settle down with them. What else lies ahead for you neither of us knows. We'll just have to wait and see what develops."

"Off and on over the years," I heard myself say, "I wished I had followed mother's footsteps and become a teacher. I've always thought teaching English would be exciting. I like children of all ages but I especially liked high school students. I talked about making a change when I was married to Rich, but he discouraged me. We had a big mortgage payment to meet and we needed the money to make the monthly payments. He made fun of my talk of teaching, calling me a dreamer. When that didn't discourage me, he called me an idealistic fool. I finally let the whole idea drop away. Back then I usually did what he wanted me to do. I wasn't very good at asserting myself. I'm still learning to live my life as if it is my own."

I fell silent then. I was surprised by my words. I had forgotten the dream. Listening to my father talk about his dreams made me remember. I did want to be a teacher.

My father interrupted my thoughts. "Years fly by so quickly," he said, "you catch them only in memory. Time passes whether you're living to the fullest or not. You have a chance now to reinvent yourself. Don't waste the opportunity. Do you understand what I'm saying?"

"I think I do," I replied. "But I need to work," I protested. "I need to bring in money to cover my share of the expenses."

"We aren't going to starve. Farmers never have any money but they always have food. We've got a house to live in that's paid for. Now is the time. Make do with less and go after things that matter. You're still young enough to find the fire. Learn from my mistakes. Don't wait until you're old. Whenever you use the word 'but' you should stop and ask yourself what you really mean. 'But' is a word that covers up a lot, including fear and lack of confidence. Think about it," he said. "Now," he said, pushing back his chair and getting ready to stand up, " I think it's time for me to go find something to do while there's still some afternoon left to do it in."

He stood up and glanced at the dishes.

"I'll do the dishes," I said, reading his mind.

"I'll do the supper dishes," he promised.

As I washed the dishes, I thought about our conversation. I wished I said some things back to him. I should have told him that he was being too hard on himself. I should have communicated the kinder, gentler view I held of him.

My father isn't perfect. True enough, I could say that. He could be an obstinate old man, set in his ways. But there were many aspects of his character I admired.

He loves the birds. He says they began to sing up the sun before daybreak. He says he can hear the robins flying to the tallest tree and trilling and singing their hearts out to make the sun peek over the horizon. He says he loves to hear the barn swallows chattering as they gather on the electrical lines running between the barn and the house, and the mourning doves cooing softly and rhythmically a little later, as they look for seeds and grain on the ground. He calls it the morning chorus. "Got to go to bed now so I can awaken in time to hear the morning chorus," he will say when he says good night. He calls bluebirds "his happiness bird." In that way, he is a sort of poet.

He likes to listen to the chorus through his half-sleep, half-wake state and then slowly come up to waking, listening for the sun's rise over the treetops on the boundaries of our farm. He says he can hear that daily miracle. He will arise then, when the sun has colored the sky a pink the petunia blossom would envy and sit on the edge of the bed. He will shove his feet into slippers and walk to the window to pull up the shade and look at the landscape he loves so much, checking the boundaries of his world. Then he is a sort of artist, admiring the way the corn is growing in neat green rows, green stripes against the black earth, stripes that widen, and obliterate the black ground to become a sea of golden tassels shining against the sword-like leaves.

When the sun catches the golden tassels just right, the field shimmers. He will call me out to the porch then, to see the ephemeral and fleeting painting. When the sun slips down a few more degrees into the horizon, it will be gone, never to be the same again. Changing, shifting, become something different the next day.

He is also a like a philosopher. He gives himself time to sit and think. He is like a bird himself, sitting there in the early morning light. His morning sound is the slurp he makes as he drinks the hot strong brew, letting it work open his mind and awaken him to the needs of the day. He ruminates about what needs to be done, how he can make best use of his time.

After breakfast, he will begin to address the needs of the day. He always says that the needs cry out to him; he does not have to think them up.

Then he becomes a man of action. His first stop is the garden, where the news there is weeds, or beetles growing fat on potato plants, or rabbits that have left droppings by the lettuce. This is the kind of news he can deal with, take some action against, and affect some change.

And so he begins to leave his mark on the world. He glances up occasionally to look about him. Bluebirds fly from field to house, feeding young, and my father is pleased that they moved into the house he built and placed for them. They have already raised one clutch and are hard at work on the next. The sun rises, and the day rises up in its own fullness. He begins to gather speed, gather news to tell me when I come out the door to go to work.

My father will make a difference in the world that no newscaster will put in his program. He is content with that, to matter only at the smallest level of existence, like an ant in an anthill, or a bird in the yard. All his hopes of glory are contained in doing each small task well, making claim to only as much as he can manage, and trusting that God will notice that his works though small in nature are nonetheless good and true and full of his moral character. His signature on the world has always been a small neat row of work done to the best of his ability without need for glory or wealth.

So I am learning from him. I have learned it doesn't have to be big, it can be small; that doesn't matter. In fact I am beginning to believe that the smaller the contribution, the more likely that no one else will stoop to do it. Others want glory, and there is no glory in small.

I have taken to walking the farm and country roads. Walking is exercise but more than that, walking is meditation. I am not in a hurry to get done with the walk once I start it, although sometimes I tell myself that I must hurry, so much is waiting for me to do. But once I start the ramble, I find that I am in the here and now and those other things calling me to action become mute.

I love to walk the farm roads, two miles of roads meandering between the boundaries of our land. I study the roadside vegetation, trying to identify the plants. I watch the birds, and occasionally see a pheasant or deer or raccoon, or skunk. I watch the land for changes in the crops. I watch the hills in the distance for subtle shifts as the seasons progress.

Sometimes I take the township road and walk to see the neighborhood. Strictly speaking, it isn't a neighborhood. Our neighbors are 80 acres away on all four sides of the farm, but I have been watching their cars come and go, spotting them occasionally biking or walking, and we are neighbors. We raise our hands in greeting, or if in the car, raise one finger from the steering wheel in what is the country version of "hello and how are you?"

One of the smallest contributions I can make is pick up roadside garbage. I find pop and beer cans, cigarette packages, wine and beer bottles, pizza boxes, wrappers from McDonald hamburgers, and Kentucky Fried Chicken containers. The trash tells me something about the eating habits of people who throw garbage out the window of their cars.

Finally, I think about how my father has gleaned wisdom from weathering life's exigencies. He knows change is the one constant. He is still changing right before my eyes and he wants me to do the same. If an old man can change, then I think to myself, "You too can change Ruthie."

Chapter Eight
Spring

My father comes into the kitchen from outdoors one March day. I can smell spring on his coat, the bright smell of sunshine and warm rain, ripening plant buds and sweet earth, mixed in a perfume that calls me to the clothesline outside. For me spring begins on that morning.

I wash winter dirt from the clotheslines, running the rag along the vinyl ropes. When I wash this rag, it will stay striped black from the grime until it has been washed several times. As I walk under the lines while my hand runs the rag along the rope, I smell piquant soil. I hear birds singing. I feel the stirrings of life all around. I linger. I have missed this ritual.

Then I search for the old clothes pin bag I stored away in a closet. Many seasons of hanging in sunshine have faded the fabric. Still, the old thing has another season of life. Wire holds the bag taut so that I can reach in for clothespins. But first the pins must be sorted.

I dump the contents onto the brown sere lawn, damp from melting snow. I throw the pins that are one piece back into the bag. I like the pins that have a spring in the middle better. But the one piece ones won't come apart and work well on towels, socks, and the thicker garments. The spring pins clamp thinner clothing better. Once the one piece ones are thrown back into the bag, I sort the pins to find the hinged ones that are whole and add them. Finally, I put pins back together, finding sets of wooden pieces and a spring for the middle. I throw away the leftovers. There are always strays, just as there are always stray socks. I remember that I bought some new pins recently and go find them. The clothespins range in color from weathered gray like some of our old sheds to new smooth pale wood that feel like silk on my fingertips.

Then I descend into the dark basement holding onto winter's chill for the wash. I climb the steps with the heavy clothesbasket containing sheets and underwear. When I emerge, bright sunshine blinds me and makes my eyes water.

Reaching for one end of the sheet, lining up the ends, then hanging the sheet with three clothespins so the breeze won't send it sailing across the yard. Reaching down for another sheet. Then pillow cases. Down one line with underwear and up the other. Repetitive work: bending, reaching, pinning, bending, reaching, pinning.

After months of being cooped up, I feel as if a prison sentence has been commuted. I am wearing my winter jacket, and my fingers will be cold from touching wet laundry in the cold, but my jacket is unzipped, my head is uncovered and my hair blows in the breeze.

Laundry will be whiter at the end of the day, smelling of earth and sun, wind and water. My mother loved to turn her face to the sun when she hung out wash. She wanted sun color on her face and arms. She loved washing this way even though it was hard work to haul heavy baskets up the steps, out to the clothes line, and then at the end of the afternoon, take the clothes down, fold them neatly, and carry them back into the house to be put away. A whiff of the clean scent as we opened the drawer would rise just as the smell of freshly baked bread rises from the pans baking in the oven. The aroma would greet us as we put the sheets on the bed, another emanation as we put on the clothes that had dried on the line, rough and stiff until softened by body heat. It was the smell of mother love I realize now that I am doing the work.

Hanging wash outside is a ritual of living life in tune with the seasons. I am happy to take it up. I am happy to do as my mother did. When I am at the clotheslines, I am myself; I am my mother, my grandmother, and my grandmother's mother. I am loving them all, honoring them in this most minute, humble way, keeping them alive in my heart by imitating their way with the laundry.

Today I hang out the wash. Maybe tomorrow it will snow. But spring has arrived once wash is hung outside for the first time.

Other spring rituals follow—washing the windows, washing bedding and hanging the comforters and quilts outside to dry in the brisk winds, flapping and dancing on the line. Dusting the corners of the house for spider webs and dust bunnies. Washing and waxing the wood floors until they gleam and glow. All the while working in outside jobs, pruning bushes, raking oak leaves that finally release their grip, plowing the garden plot, raking it smooth, pushing wheel barrows of compost to the garden and to flower beds to renew the soil.

The inconsistency of spring weather is good. Winter makes a body sluggish and slowed down. I start a job with energy then realize I am not in the same shape I was at summer's end. I feel tired, sleepy, my blood too thick. The good days alternating with bad weather give me time to harden, build myself back up for physical labor and warmer temperatures.

All these tasks are done with a light heart, matching the ever-lengthening days, all of this reminding me that nature renews itself and so should we. I will be renewed when I touch the black, loamy soil and become intimate with Mother Nature, like a woman who has returned to her lover and feels his skin with her fingertips as they lie together naked in bed.

Spring makes me yearn for a different kind of love, the love from a man, someone who would brush the hair out of my eyes at the end of a long day, and tell me everything will be all right. Someone who would see me forking manure and think I was beautiful. Someone who would bring me a cup of coffee in the morning. Someone to lie down with after a long hard day, where we would exist together, breathing in, breathing out, listening to each other, knowing we need not waste our breath on words, and his body heat would come over to me and we would fall asleep in our own private world, safe in the knowledge that we had been claimed and loved.

The yearning was a tension. It was beneath everything I did. Yearning, watching, waiting, but not having it happen, not this spring, maybe next year, I would hope, sighing to myself, going on with my life, thinking of Charlie, for whom the season of spring empty of this love stretched out the length of his life.

I assumed it would be I who found love. One evening after supper when I was working in the kitchen, the sound of my father talking came drifting into the room. I called out, "What? I can't hear you. The water is running."

His voice continued. Now he was laughing. I felt annoyed. I walked into the living room. He was talking on the telephone. When I entered the room, he turned his back to me. He was murmuring into the phone, in a low melodious voice. I realized that he did not want me to hear what he was saying. I felt offended in some way that I did not understand. I went back to the kitchen.

A little later he came back to the kitchen. He had changed clothes, combed his hair, and was ready to go out. "I've got an appointment," he said. "I won't stay out too late."

I looked up from the sink in amazement, but by then his long legs had taken him past me, and he was descending the steps by the back door racing to the shed where he parked his truck. I realized that he was in a hurry to see someone.

I smelled another woman and I felt outrage. He was being disloyal to my mother, who had been dead for three years. I was also angry, because he had done this without checking with me first. I could feel the nice easy rapport we had established totter under the weight of this development. Who did he think he was, anyway, I found myself thinking. Tomorrow we would have to have a talk.

But the next day, I had cooled down. All I asked was, "Who is the lucky lady?"

My father answered, "I'm not ready to tell you."

I could feel a look of hurt cross my face, though I tried to suppress it.

"Don't take offense," he said. "All I mean is that it might be nothing, or it might be everything. I need to take a little time, and when I think I know if I want this, then I will tell you."

I turned away. "Fine," I said, "Have it your way."

I nursed the grudge for a few days. I wasn't my usual talkative self, and avoided spending time with him. He gave no signs of changing his mind, nor even that he had noticed my chilly attitude.

He left one evening in the same manner as the first time.

I watched him walking across the lawn to his truck, a spring in his step, a happy tilt to his head, and I realized that this was another way in which he was changing. Some day I too might want to change in a new and different way. I didn't feel I needed his permission to find new friends and interests. Maybe he didn't feel he needed mine. I would wait for him to tell me more.

Chapter Nine
Spring Unfolds

We are watching the fields for signs that frost is leaving, that soon we can work the ground. Snow patches are shrinking. Wet spots are drying.

We have a dozen different soil types on the farm. Each has their own characteristics, readying for planting at different speeds. Sandy soil dries first. Clay holds wet. During a long dry spell the sandy ground we were able to work earlier than the clay will leave the crops thirsty for water. There are advantages and disadvantages to each type.

Names of the different soil series for our farm are exotic: Ludington and Humbird, Plainfield and Friendship, Morocco and Billett, Meridian and Arland, Kert and Newsom, Menagha, Shiffer and Vesper. Each series is named for a town or other important feature near the place where the soil series was first observed and mapped.

Soil is a mixture of particles that range from sand to silt to clay. If I had learned the continuum of particles as a schoolgirl, I might have sung a song as I jumped rope on the playground with my friends. I would have called out in a sweet girlish voice the range of soil mixtures: "Sand, loamy sand, sandy loam, loam, silt, silt loam, sandy clay, loam, clay loam, silty clay loam, sandy clay, silty clay, clay" as I jumped while my friends swung the rope harder and faster, trying to trip me.

The return of sand hill cranes is a sign of spring. When I hear the clacking sound they make for the first time in the spring, my heart opens as wide with happiness as if a beloved member of the family is returning. Cranes mate for life. Each year the couple returns to breed and raise their young, though they shift the location of the nest from year to year. Each morning and evening, I hear the sound of their cry as they fly back home from feeding elsewhere.

In early summer, I will spot only the male eating in the fields. When their young one is old enough to feed along side its parents, I will find the family together eating soybeans and corn. Even when I am inside, I hear the cranes calling to each other, making a sound like wooden sticks being knocked together, like castanets.

I enjoy the role we play in their life, providing them with a safe home. Their return gives me a feeling of being solidly in my world, like my father's footsteps on the floor, or his laugh as he tells a joke. We share a world and their return to our world means everything is right in that world.

One evening spring peepers sing from the wet marsh. They have emerged from deep in the earth where they remained lifeless all winter. They begin singing at dusk and sing into the night. Now I know spring is here to stay.

Soon wildflowers and trees and shrubs will flower. By Mother's Day, white trilliums in the woods dot undergrowth in patches. Wetland marsh marigolds color the ground a cheerful yellow. Wild cherry and dogwood in the fence lines and road ditches paint a haze on the strips between fields and along the road, delicate and fragrant. The tender beauty will wind up and down hedgerows as far as my eye can see.

Birds return and set up camp. Bluebirds first, then robins. Blackbirds come back to the wetlands, sitting on dead cattails, singing loudly to mark their territory. In mass, the red-winged blackbirds fly to our yard for food. The din of their song nearly drowns out my own thoughts.

One day barn swallows reappear, a few scouts at first, then the whole flock. They swoop and capture insects, flying gracefully like fighter pilots through open barn windows to make their way back to their old nests.

A killdeer comes to check out the gravel we dumped on wet spots in the driveway. If need be, if the bird persists, we will throw loose hay over the gravel to discourage the female from nesting there.

We plant our garden early. First are green peas. We set a row of old stock panels, tied together with used bailing twine, between metal stakes for tendrils to grab for their climb up the wire. One old wives' tale says snow has to fall on peas three times before spring will warm. Another says it's robins' toes. The earlier peas are planted, the better.

Sweet peas need to be planted while the ground is cold as well. I love the fragrance of sweet peas, as sweet as a lover's breath. They flower in soft colors—pinks, purples, blues-- like pastels painted by a fairy. They possess old-fashioned loveliness, not flashy nor bright, but muted, like old maids who've tamed their passions and wear soft silks.

We alternate from year to year between green peas, the ones that require hand shelling, and Chinese pea pods that are used whole after stringing. Green peas are labor intensive. If we planted them yearly, I think we would stop. But one year's absence is long enough to make our memories dim. When I am ordering seed, I'll think, "This year I need some green peas. Chinese peas are good, but green peas are better."

Midway through the season, memory has improved. There is no fast way to shell peas by hand. You have to sit yourself down on the porch in a comfortable chair, with a pile of peas in front of you, and a bowl between your legs, and do the work. First pull off the string that runs down the pod, unzipping them. Then use your thumb to break open the pod, dislodging peas inside.

My father can be talked into shelling peas, but mid-season, even his patience is worn thin. I'll join him then, shelling my mountain of pea pods as he works on his.

Despite my beginning resistance to the job, it's the kind of work that soothes you, the plunk of the first peas hitting the bowl, then the mound growing and growing. We eat the early ones cooked with butter, but the later ones are reserved for creamed peas on toast, the cream sauce made with real butter, and whole milk. One or two slices of creamed peas on toast seem like fair reward for the work and fuss.

My father believes that potatoes should be planted on Good Friday. The local mill has a stock of potatoes. When the beds are ready— the friable ground plowed, the trenches lying open—we make a run to the feed mill to add to our supply of sprouted potatoes from the root cellar. We try to guess how many we need as we load brown paper bags with the seed potatoes, a few of this variety, more of that one. When we get back home, we find we have bought too many, so we add more rows to the potato patch.

Then we plant onions, three varieties, red, white, and yellow. Onions will be mature by the end of July. In a few weeks, we start pulling the first green ones. When onions begin to gain size, we can use them freely. The foliage dies back in late summer. We pull the onions and lay them on pallets under cover to dry. In September, I will put on gloves, pull off dried tops, separate the good from the bad, and put them in bags. Then they hang from nails in the garage until nights have become cold enough to worry about freezing. We take them to the basement to hang in a dark, dry corner. Onions last all winter. We use the red ones first, like potatoes, then the yellow, and finally the white. Our soil, rich with nutrients from compost, grows onions so pungent I cry at the chopping board.

Then the radishes and lettuce are seeded. Radishes come up in a week, and by three weeks, something fresh and good from the earth can be eaten. They will be crisp, snap under our teeth, my tongue tingling from their bite. I eat them with salt. Sometimes I eat a dozen as I stand at the sink and cut off roots and tops while washing them under cold running water before submersing them in a bowl of cold water.

I seed the lettuce in succession, two weeks apart, until I have half a row of various varieties, Black seeded Simpson, a red leaf, a green leaf lettuce. When the entire half row has matured, we will be drowning in green leafy things. A taco salad, a wilted salad, a layered salad, they won't begin to touch the bounty.

Now we are watching rhubarb. Rhubarb grows without any help from us, although mulching under the plants with old hay slices keeps grass from growing into the beds. We have twenty-five feet of rhubarb, more rhubarb than we could possibly eat.

Rhubarb is a spring tonic and rite. I watch for tender young shoots to emerge. When there are enough, I make a sauce, rhubarb chopped fine, sugar, water, boiled together for a few minutes, then left to sit. Simple pleasure. It takes a batch or two to get the proportion right. First too runny, or too sour, or too sweet. But a short practice run will make my hands and eyes coordinate the three ingredients. We eat the sauce as dessert, as a side dish, as a topping for ice cream. I make batch after batch. My father wants me to freeze some, and I will to humor him, but rhubarb tastes best after months of deprivation. Anticipation is part of the treat.

Then I move on to rhubarb Jell-O jam made from my grandmother's recipe. I wrote out the recipe card in my girlish hand many years ago when I stayed with her and we made the jam together. The flavor of the jam depends on the Jell-O. Strawberry is our favorite, but I use orange, raspberry, apricot, and peach. There are so many varieties of Jell-O today that I know my grandmother would be churning out a batch in every flavor if she were still alive. Lots of sugar makes it sweet. I am still under the belief that I can make use of all the rhubarb in the patch. Then, one day I look down the row of tall stalks and know I have been defeated.

Rhubarb needs to replenish itself by growing untouched. Two good months, part of May, all of June, most of July, before it becomes stringy and bug-eaten. Rhubarb should not be harvested after July 31. I am relieved when the end of July comes. Now I can let it grow without thoughts of being wasteful. All I do now is keep watch for pesky seed heads that must be snapped off before they sap the roots of energy.

Lilacs bloom at the end of May. We have an abundance of lilacs, bunches of them, rows of them, hedges of them. Charlie's mother loved lilacs. There are some of the common variety, in both purple and white, and some French lilacs, curlier and deeper colored than their country cousin. I love them all. Lilacs bushes are good bird habitat. They will be full of nests as the season progresses.

When they are in bloom, the fragrance lies over the farm like a cloud. I pick bouquets of them for the house where they scent inside as well. They drink all the water in the vase and fall wilted to the table. I replenish them daily. There are seven, maybe ten, good days of lilac blooms. Then they're overly mature, browning at the edges. Their nectar attracts bees now.

One warm sunny day I retrieve the hammock from storage to hang between two Locust trees perfectly spaced for a hammock. On that day, summer begins.

Summer heat burns my yearning for love out of my bones. Only the memory of the yearning lingers.

One evening my father invites his new woman friend for supper. He cooks his specialty, one that I love because he learned it from my mother, the way she cooked a pot roast in the old electric cooker until it fell apart under your fork. He mashes potatoes the way my mother mashed potatoes. He cooks carrots the way my mother cooked carrots. But when the woman comes, a plump gray haired woman with a soft gentle smile and twinkling brown eyes, I find it hard to hold it against her that she is eating the cooking my father learned from my mother.

She is so nervous in my presence that she spills her milk as she reaches to pass me the meat. And I suddenly see how I must look to her, stern-faced, judging, wanting everything to stay the same for me. I soften but can't immediately let go of possessive feelings. All I can do is offer to wash the dishes so that they can go relax on the front porch. When they get up and leave the kitchen, I sit at the table for a moment, feeling sorry for myself, but then Eloise surprises me by coming back in.

"I felt guilty. I told Arlan that I had to come back and help you. I always told my children that many hands make light work." She is smiling at me.

"Do you want to wash or dry?" I answer. I discover I am smiling back at her.

Chapter Ten

Not in our Backyard

When I lived in the city, I never thought much about where mail was delivered. Now that I live in the country, our mailbox is across the road from the farm at the end of our long driveway.

Every afternoon my father comes in for an afternoon break. My first question is, "Did you get the mail?"

"No," he'll say, "but I can if you want."

I look at his weary face. "No, I'll go," I answer. I put on a jacket, boots if I need them, and trudge down the long driveway to the road. As soon as I'm outside, I enjoy it but enjoyment doesn't prevent me from hoping mail has come.

I look both ways for traffic, and cross to the mailbox. If I'm lucky, mail has arrived. It will be sitting inside the box, nestled to the side. If not, I look down the road to see if I can see the mailman's red car with the flashing light on top. If I can't, I go back to the house. Then I repeat the ritual in a little while.

Today I trekked down the driveway for the mail. When I opened the squeaky door, mail was waiting. I gave a satisfied sigh.

I shuffled through the letters on my way back to the house. A business envelope with the county Zoning and Planning Department in the return address made me hurry. A letter with a government return address could complicate life.

I dumped the mail onto the kitchen table. My father was enjoying his cup of fresh coffee, making satisfied slurping sounds.

I ripped open the letter, and then gave an involuntary shout.

"What's wrong?" he immediately asked.

I read a little more.

"Now that you've got me worried, you've got to tell me what the letter says."

I pulled myself away from reading long enough to answer. "It seems they want to rezone the old Haffield farm from Agriculture-One to Agriculture-Two."

"You don't say," my father said, sounding as perturbed as I felt. "We'll just see about that. If land is zoned Agriculture-One, it takes 35 acres to build a house. If it's Agriculture-Two, the requirement drops to 20 acres. Maybe they want to build one of them fancy country estates with big houses on lots of acres."

I passed the letter over to him. He read it silently. "Son of a gun," he said, when he had finished with the letter, "I wonder what's up. I haven't heard anything about the land being for sale."

"We'll have to fight it," I said.

"When's that hearing again?"

"Tomorrow night at the County Courthouse in the Commission chambers."

"Well that hardly gives us time to get organized," he said. He thought a moment. "Call John and Sally and see if they've heard anything."

John and Sally owned some vacant land further down the road on the other side of the Haffield property. They planned to build a house on it some day, but for now, they lived in town. Sally ran one of local restaurants. John worked fulltime but he often helped Sally out at the restaurant.

The land in question was across the road from our farm. The paper mill in Clear Water owned the land. They had bought it ten years ago from the Haffield widow after her husband committed suicide. The paper mill had planned to dump sludge but before they'd had a chance, Rush River Township passed stiff land use laws because of concerns about the effects of the sludge on the aquifer. The old farm fronted county forestland and the river. Charlie had told us about the fight over sludge dumping when we bought the farm.

Teenagers were constantly vandalizing the old house when they had beer-drinking parties after dark on the property. The result was doors off their hinges and broken out windows attracting rats and raccoons to the shelter inside. With each passing year, the buildings looked more and more rundown.

It was a pretty location though. Sitting at the end of a dead-end dirt road, next to forest and the river, the place was more quiet and serene than our farm. I tried to imagine what a cozy little place it had once been. I'd heard that the sandy soil was marginal at best for farming so none of the farmers had wanted to buy it but it seemed a shame that the farm had been bought up by the paper mill rather than someone who liked hunting and fishing.

I looked up John and Sally's number in the phone book. My father stood beside me while I dialed.

"Hello," John answered.

"Hi John, this is Ruth Joseph. Do you remember me? My father and I bought old Charlie's farm a few years ago."

"Of course I do. How are you doing?" he asked gustily.

"Well, we're fine, but we just got a letter from the county zoning commission about the old Haffield farm. They want to rezone it from Ag-One to Ag-Two. Did you get a letter and do you know what's going on?"

"No, I don't think we got one, but we should have. Our land is right on the other side. Do you know what's up?"

"No, we don't. That's why I'm calling. I was hoping you knew something. Sally talks to a lot of people at the restaurant. Tomorrow night there's a hearing at the court house."

"Well Sally and I will make a point of being there. I'll see what I can find out. I work in the court house, you know, so I'll go talk to them first thing in the morning."

"Okay, well, I guess we'll see you tomorrow night."

I hung up. My father was shaking his head. "Everybody around the property should have gotten a letter. I don't understand it at all."

The phone rang. I answered it. My father was still standing next to me.

"Ruth, this is John. I just looked through the mail. We got a letter too but I didn't look at the mail today. I put it on top of the refrigerator til I had more time. I'll ask around tomorrow and give you a call as soon as I hear anything."

The next morning right after we had come in from doing chores, the phone rang. "You get it," my father said, "it might be John."

"Hello," I said.

John said. "This is what I found out. "There are several radio controlled airplane clubs in Clear Water. One of them lost their lease a few years ago and has been trying to find a place for a landing strip ever since. No one wants them because the planes are noisy. I guess there have been a series of zoning fights. The club president knows the manager of the paper company. They're going to let the club use the land. I guess they've already had it surveyed because they want to build a landing strip right down the middle of one of the fields. But they can't build the landing strip unless the zoning is changed. Sally and I will be there for sure. We'll meet you in the hearing room."

"Okay then, we'll see you in a little while," I answered. I hung up.

John and Sally, my father and I showed up at the meeting about the same time. Club members packed the room. I had a sick feeling in the pit of my stomach. We weren't prepared to stage much of a fight. Club members far outnumbered us. We sat quietly as the meeting was called to order.

But in a lucky break, he zoning committee lacked a quorum. The chairman of the committee was apologetic. He asked if we would wait for a few minutes while someone tried to track down the missing member. While we waited, I said a silent prayer. A few minutes later the chairman reported that the missing member couldn't be found. He informed us that they would meet again next week and consider the matter at that time. We four looked at each other in relief.

We walked to our cars. We didn't want to talk inside where our conversation could be overheard by the club members. Sally had an idea, "I'll start circulating a petition. A lot of people come eat at my restaurant. I can gather signatures against the change before the next hearing.

"That's sounds great," my father said. "Ruth and I will call all the neighbors around the property. We'll see how many we can get to attend the hearing in person. Let's see, there's old man Kramer and his son. They like to deer hunt. I don't think they'd appreciate all the noise and commotion from the planes scaring away the wild life. There's the Webber family up the road. They might be against it. And then there's Annie and Russ Farnsworth up the other way. She raises horses. I guess she grew up on their place and she probably won't like all the noise either."

"Don't forget about her mother," John suggested. "She lives across the road from them."

"Isn't she that religious nut?" my father asked, "the one that they thought was writing threatening letters to the funeral homes in the area because they embalm?"

"That's the one. Everyone is afraid of her, but she's still a voter."

"Well, I guess we could call her then," my father answered.

I was remembering her as a big-boned woman who wore her long hair up in a bun, long dresses, and dark capes in colder weather. She gave off a creepy feeling every time I ran into her in town.

I felt more optimistic now that we had a plan. As soon as we got home, we got busy. My father offered to telephone the neighbors. They were uninformed about the change, but once he had filled them in, most said they'd try to make it to the meeting, even the religious woman. A few days before the hearing, we called John and Sally to find out how they'd done on their petition drive.

"We've got eight-two names," Sally told me. "John's been down to the zoning office several times. They told him the county commission doesn't like a big fuss over a zoning change so we stand a good chance of beating it."

"I hope you're right," I said.

At the next meeting of the zoning committee, our group had gotten bigger. Now the opposition included my father and me, Sally and John, the old man and his son who liked to hunt, and Annie and Russ who had horses. Their mother sent her regrets. She'd been called to pray over someone's sickbed. Not everyone we had called was against it, but they didn't show up in favor either. Sally and John brought their petition. Now the list had grown to one hundred names.

The club made a presentation full of promises-- members wouldn't be flying everyday; they wouldn't disturb farm fields; noise from the planes was exaggerated.

 My father punched me in the ribs. "Heck, half them old coots have lost their hearing so they can't hear a darn thing." I looked over the club members. They seemed to be a group of old men. Even though they were pushing their hobby as a family affair, it looked like owning a radio-controlled airplane was something you needed a retiree's time and money to enjoy.

We waited in suspense while the zoning committee took a vote. "Opposed," said the first member.

"Opposed." said the second.

'I'm going to abstain," the chairman announced.

"In favor," the next one said.

"In favor," the last member voted.

Without a majority, the request was denied.

We were jubilant. We had won.

The next day I hurried down to the mailbox to get the mail and the newspaper. I opened the newspaper eagerly to read the report about the hearing but I quickly cried out, surprised.

"What's wrong now?" my father asked.

"That can't be," I said. "We were there."

"What can't be?" my father asked.

"They're reporting that the vote passed.

"Call John," my father ordered.

John said he'd go down personally to see what the zoning office said. It didn't take long for him to call us back. "That's what the zoning office is saying as well. Someone changed their mind."

Now I was mad. "I'm calling the chairman," I said. I looked in the phone book for the number of the chairman. Sure enough, he was listed. I called him at home.

He answered the phone. I questioned him. "But who changed their mind?" I asked.

"I did," he answered, "so the motion to rezone carried."

I argued with him but he said it was legal to change an abstention. During the conversation, he let slip that the county board would have to vote on the zoning change before it was final, unless the township got involved and voted against it. If they voted against the zoning change before it went to the full county board, the issue would more than likely be dead. The county could overrule the township on zoning matters but seldom did. I hung up with that valuable nugget of information.

"We will be able to block it, it seems, if we can get the township to vote against it before the county commission meets to consider the matter," I told my father, who had been standing by me as I talked on the phone.

"Well, let's do it then," my father urged.

I called the members of our town board to oppose the zoning request. Two of them were farmers like us. The third had been a farmer but now worked in a factory, farming part-time. My father called the neighbors and asked them to call the township board members. We asked to be put on the agenda for the next meeting, which fortuitously would be the day before the county commission met, in the nick of time to stop the zoning change.

The town hall is located in the middle of Rush River rather than in the countryside. It had been over run by city life years before. The building is more than a hundred years old, one room with a stage at the far end of the room for the board to sit, along with the secretary and treasurer. The secretary and treasurer are paid positions. The rest of the board, two members and a chairman, run for election every two years. The citizens sit below on long hard wooden benches painted ship's gray. There are no restrooms in the town hall, but we do have heat.

Last winter a chimney fire in the old wood stove threatened to burn the building down. The wood stove was replaced with a large electric heater. It's too hot in winter, and in summer, big fans set around on the floor to cool off the room only add to the noise without making it any cooler. Creaking from the old wooden floor is over powering. The entire building is full of noise. The floor creates a loud din when someone walks across it. The old windows bounce voices off the walls so that they reverberate around the room like boomerangs. Benches squeak as butts shift to find a more comfortable position. It is nearly impossible to hear unless you sit up front and pay close attention.

At the township board meeting, the president of the radio controlled airplane club came alone, unaccompanied by his usual coterie of club members. My father whispered to me, "He's an arrogant son of a gun. He thinks he can waltz in here and speak without going through the motion of getting on the agenda. Well, we'll just see what's in store for him."

I listened hard to hear the town chairman tell him that the meeting was for the township residents. If there's any time left after they spoke, then he could have some time to present his side.

The meeting was called to order. After conducting regular business, the rezoning request came up. The neighbors stood one by one and spoke their piece against changing the zoning to allow the landing strip. They argued that changing the zoning from A-1 to A-2 not only broadened the types of businesses that could use the land, but reduced the minimum lot size. Even if we hadn't been opposed the use of the land for the radio controlled landing strip, we would have objected because of the long term ramifications of changing the zoning classification. Very little land is ever rezoned back to more restrictive usage. We all knew that.

John and Sally spoke at the end. They presented the petition to the town board. "None of them will dare make that many residents upset," my father whispered in my ear. I turned around to see what the club president thought of all this. But he was gone. During the discussion, he had quietly left the meeting.

The chairman called the question, and the voting began.

"Opposed," said the first board member.

"Opposed," said the second board member.

"Opposed," said the third board member.

 The vote was unanimous.

The chairman instructed the town clerk to type up the resolution and hand deliver it to the county board office the next day before the commission met to consider the matter. Now we had really won.

Still, just to be on the safe side, a bunch of us attended the county board hearing to make sure they denied the request. We all breathed easier after the vote. We talked in a tight knot out in the parking lot. We agreed we had to work together to keep it the way we liked it, undeveloped and a quiet rural neighborhood.

Though a small victory in the fight against development encroaching upon rural life, we enjoyed the sweet taste of victory. And we rekindled the spirit of neighborliness that had been flagging on our road. By banding together, we rekindled it. We vowed to keep the spirit alive.

When picnic weather arrived, my father and I hosted the first annual neighborhood picnic. I made up a batch of beef barbecues and asked everyone to bring a dish to pass. We set up chairs in the front yard, and filled the coolers with beer and pop. We got better acquainted. We swapped stories, swatted mosquitoes, and listened to tall tales about hunting.

Now when we passed each other on the road, we raised our index finger off the steering wheel in greeting. That said it all," Hello. Nice to see you. I'm doing fine. Hope you are the same."

But in our heart of hearts, my father and I knew it was a temporary victory. We could put out small fires, but one day the line between country and city would blur until one day the only thing left would be old farm houses mixed with new subdivisions and expensive country homes. The very thing that attracted people to move to the country in the first place would be destroyed by their coming.

Chapter Eleven
A Season of Ease

It feels as if we will always live surrounded by waving fields of lush green crops, and colorful blooming flowers. Soft summer breezes play through the trees. Birds make beautiful music as we sit on the front porch, our living room for the season.

The hammock hangs between honey locust trees in the front yard. Under their lacy leaves, I relax. Up above is sky with leaf patterns on cerulean blue. I lie back and dream, watching birds fly overhead, weaving through the lace, perching, listening, singing, taking off for flight, returning, and further up, the contrails from air planes leaving white silky threads that slowly spread out until they disappear into the deep blue sea of sky. The long pods of the honey locust form slowly as the days pass, not yet black and crooked, rattling and shaking through winter storms.

I take time outs in the hammock, on the porch, ruminating about the questions my father had raised.

"Where was this path going? Who was I? "

Taking inventory, considering myself as if I were not myself, but someone else who had come to me for advice. Trying to put my outward life in tune with my inner life, with the person I had once been before I lost track of her. I was slowly relaxing into a different pace, where life was tied to the rhythm and beat of Mother Nature, to farm business, not the race to beat last year's sales, last year's profit. Giving up the need to be in control of every aspect of life.

On rare days, simply being, like I was on a long summer vacation. Sometimes I felt transported back to childhood, back to summer recess, when I had the child's privilege of living as if there were no bigger world outside our family's home. My father's presence seemed to bring that all back. Sleepily, lazily, I would awaken on a summer day and feel safe and secure again.

Time alone was plentiful. Hoeing in the garden, riding the tractor while pulling the mower down the hayfield, the tractor manifesting a power that thrilled me. Washing and blanching vegetables for the freezer, my busy hands freeing my mind to go on its voyage of discovery.

We were two peas in a pod. My father relished his time alone as well. We came together at meals, for conversation, for sharing, then parted like lions on a hunt. It was a good feeling, to have this companionship, yet the freedom to be alone as well. My obligations to him were not of a wife, and as his daughter, I had his unending affection. I was nestled down in his love, enjoying every moment, and finding it easy to return.

The best thinking came when I was observing other worlds, watching the corn sprout, grow from seedling to sturdy plant, tassel, set ears, yellow corn silk emerging then darkening to a rusty brown. Sitting quietly, watching the fields. Deer moving stealthily in the corn and soybeans. Sand hill cranes feeding on soybeans with their baby. Wild turkeys and pheasant claiming gleaning rights. Hawks seizing prey. Hummingbirds dancing to attract a mate.

Creatures going about daily activities just like my father and me, finding food, shelter, raising their babies. We lived on parallel planes with other worlds.

My senses began to teach me that there is rhythm and flow to life bigger, broader, wider than my small life had been aware of. I was awakening to the universe.

I felt inconsequential yet, if I were to throw a rock into the small stream that flowed in the corner of the farm, the rock would cause ripples. So would my life, I was beginning to see.

What ripples did I want my days on this earth to produce? Pondering as my hands and body worked, as I rested and watched, I found answers.

Yes, I wanted to teach. That dream of mine was not foolish. Farming was a nice way to live, but I would not always be so easily satisfied with its demands. I had learned so much about farming already that I could see the challenge becoming less as I was able to make educated and informed decisions.

My father was a good teacher and I had learned a great deal about farming. He told me that I had it in my blood to farm. Maybe he was right. I could almost see the shadows of the long line of farmers we had come down from, his father, his father's father who had come over from Germany. I could imagine the line of peasant farmers back in the old country, raising their crops, raising their chickens. Listening to the land over centuries had become part of my make up.

But I had my mother in me too. She had loved teaching. It had brought her satisfaction and joy. I knew she had risen eagerly each morning to go teach. Her mother had been a teacher as well. I had listened to my grandmother's stories of teaching in a one-room school. We had driven by it as children for years before it had finally been torn down.

The biggest obstacle was to become qualified to teach. I would need schooling to qualify for a teaching license for high school English and I would have to do an internship. But when I discussed this with my father, he shrugged it off.

"So what," he would say. "You're smart. You always did well in school. Go for it, if that's what you want."

So I made the necessary applications.

We had a little party when I was accepted for the fall term. My sisters and brother and their families came out for a big family picnic. My oldest sister surprised me with her thoughts.

"Mom would be proud of you," she said. "She always told me she thought you should have gone into teaching."

"I didn't know that," I told her. "Why didn't she ever tell me that?"

"Ruthie, don't you remember? You always were so pigheaded, so sure you knew what you were doing. She believed in letting her children find their own way."

I looked at my father for confirmation. He nodded his head and smiled. "She was more sly than you gave her credit for," he said.

Once I had made that decision and plans, I turned to summer with all its delights.

The days ahead stretched full of so much promise as I wrung pleasure out of every moment. When the weather is good, it seems like there will never be another day with rain or snow. It seems as if time has been frozen and we will keep on doing what we are doing on this perfect day. When the weather is perfect, it is like a passionate embrace we want to hold onto forever.

How the crops grow is out of our hands now. Mother Nature is the boss. She will deal us a crop on her terms, no matter what we think.

It feels as if I have more control in the vegetable and flower garden. I can weed, spray and dust for insects and disease, water when the ground is dry.

The feel of the earth is part of the love affair. The soil kisses my fingers. I do not mind the dirt under my fingernails. The look and smell of earth, black, crumbly, smelling of decay and life at the same time, the feel of the soil, textured with clay, humus, and sand. I kneel on its soft surface, the soil molding to the shape of my kneecap, cupping it gently. Soil is as full of living things as the world above the ground. Earth worms and night crawlers, micro flora, bacteria, fungi, molds, helping the rhizomes on the plant roots obtain the necessary nutrients; the hairy ends of the rhizomes taking in water; fungi, molds, and bacteria consuming dead plant debris and transforming it back to soil.

The flowers in the yard begin blooming like beautiful actresses in a play put on in scenes. Lily of the valley takes the stage first. The flowerbed surrounding the front porch has a thick growth. I watch the pips emerge and the flowers pop from the center. I recall the children's song "White coral bells, upon a slender stock, lilies of the valley deck my garden walk." Even though the tune calls for my voice to go into a range I have difficulty with, I sometimes sing this song to myself. They are delicate bells hanging from the top of long green slender stems, a little clapper hidden within the drooping flower.

I pick five or six stalks of the lily of the valley and put them into a painted vase that I especially love. The vase belonged to my grandmother, hand painted by one of her friends. It's funny how odd memories resurface. Her name was Ruby. She was a skinny wizened thing with a high cackling laugh, straw-like hair that stuck out. She chained smoked, taking a drag on her cigarette as she squinted at her work. But she was an artist.

She touched the vase with the paintbrush loaded with shades of red and pink. She'd dab, screw up her eyes and glare at the vase, hold it out and dab some more. In a few minutes, what emerged was something beautiful. When my grandmother died, my mother took the vase, and now I have it to fill with lily of the valley and place in my bedroom by the nightstand. When I fall asleep on those nights, I tell myself I am sure to have sweet dreams.

Then the purple chive flowers that grow from the big mounds of dark green spikes take the stage. I cut some of these spikes, chop the long hollow green stems into little pieces, and mix them with baked or mashed potatoes, make a special batter bread that uses the herb to impart a mild onion-like flavor to the bread.

Then snow-on-the mountain, a leafy ground cover of green and white leaves, sends up stalks of lacy flowers, next to the yellow primroses and daisies. Peonies next. Peonies smell like sweet cinnamon. They will bloom ten days, and then the blossoms will explode and lie spent on the ground next to the dark green angular-shaped foliage.

Then it seems like the show changes quickly: celosia forming red cock's combs, orange-striped tiger lilies, day lilies in orange, purple hostas that hummingbirds love, aromatic oregano flowers, two kinds of monardi— purple and red—that attract bees, rudbeckias in bright pink and with black centers, mums in white and yellow, and purple liatrus spikes. I am a grateful audience, applauding each show of beauty. Sadly, there is no intermission to catch one's breath, to stand back and drink in each scene. It rushes by too quickly.

In the vegetable garden, I grow zinnias, marigolds, and gladiolus mixed with the food, food for the spirit and food for the flesh side by side. I cultivate the flowers with the Troybilt rototiller when I am cultivating vegetables. When I have time, I hand weed as well, but not until I've done the vegetables. I always find time to weed the flowers. The sun may be setting, mosquitoes gnawing at my flesh with their pincer-like mouths, but I want to make the flowers shine out in the vegetable world. Maybe our vegetables do even better because we have flowers to dazzle them as they grow simple goodness.

It is the jewel-like hues of zinnias, the bright red, orange, yellow, purple and pink that I love. As they grow, the plant becomes stocky, branching out, sending forth new blossoms continuously. Zinnias don't smell sweet, but their blossoms last on the plant and in the vase. Even if I am not pleased by the smell, bees are pleased and come to drink. As the zinnias grow old, their stamen and pistol grow more defined, lifting up from the flower, creating stars to contrast with the color of the petals.

Marigolds are stinky, but they are so bright and cheerful in their yellow, gold, and brown tones. As dusk descends, they look almost fluorescent. They grow even better when the weather cools down, and like mums, continue well into the autumn, standing up to frost after frost until the final killing one finally ends the show.

I love the ritual of taking up my scissors and going out to the garden to cut flowers for house bouquets. I will make up the bouquet as I go, snipping zinnias in different colors and then go to the perennial beds, stealing a flower from the snow on the mountain greenery, a daisy or two, a carnation, a peony, and bring the bunch into the house.

Then I decide on the vase. I have a dozen vases. Clear crystal. Blown glass in blue, green, or pink. Etched clear glass. Cut glass. Mercury glass. Molded glass. Tall. Short. Squat. Wide. Flat.

The nights hold their own with summer days, a dusky counterweight to the luminosity of sky and sunshine. I have windows flung wide open. On some nights, when it is cooler, I can feel the coolness settle down on the land, rising up to the window, creeping into the room. On those nights, I will snuggle down into my covers, extracting warmth, making a nest for myself, in the chilly night air. On other nights, when it is hot and dry, the room having been heated like an oven by the end of the day, the hot air in the room will not let cooler air enter until early morning.

On hot nights, I will throw back all the bed coverings, and open the windows as wide as they will open. The overhead fan will blow a breeze, and I will lie there smelling the flower scents as they rise in the night up to the window, picking out the monardi from the carnations. Then, after I have drifted to sleep, the night will start to cool off, and by morning, I will have grabbed the sheet and will wake shivering, the sheet wrapped around me as tight as the shroud on an Egyptian mummy. I groped for warmer covers in the night but they had fallen to the wooden floor, spilling out like waves lapping the shores of a sand beach.

Sometimes it does not cool off. A hot day without air conditioning in an old farmhouse is like living in a factory, followed by a hot night that is like sleeping in a steam bath. I watch anxiously for signs of cooling down or rain signaling a change in the weather. I greet the change eagerly, even though I know with each cool down, summer is slipping away.

My favorite month of summer is June. June is like a baby's bottom, smooth, soft. Wind, rain, drought, insects, these have not yet marred the fresh green leaves. June beauty is pristine, fresh, like teenage beauty.

The iridescent blue of barn swallows makes the birds look as if they are dressed in satin evening dress. My father and I often sit in the back yard as the sun starts its descent to watch swallows dive through open barn windows graceful and sure. They swoop around us, consuming mosquitoes and gnats. We hardly suffer from mosquitoes because of the swallows.

While we eat supper, the electric wires that run from the barn to the house will be full of them, chattering and gathering like families at their evening meal. We try to count their numbers, but just as we get to one hundred, something will cause them to rise up in a black cloud, and fly off on in their pursuit of insects. When we mow, swallows often follow behind, swooping down, catching insects that fly into the air as the mower blade fells grass blades.

By the end of June, the garden is producing more than we can eat. We'll eat five or six vegetables for supper so that nothing will be wasted. Maybe zucchini and onions sautéed in olive oil, along with lettuce salad, fresh radishes, garden peas, maybe some early Chioggia beets, a batch of kale steamed or sautéed.

By mid-July, I'm hungry for potatoes so I'll start peeking under the plants to pull out a handful of new potatoes to steam along with green beans, small baby beets, and small baby carrots. This is a good time for the garden, plenty to eat but I am not overwhelmed.

All that changes towards the end of July. We hunger for the first early tomatoes, but then we are over-run with tomatoes, cucumbers, green beans, and beets. I will work into the evening cleaning vegetables, blanching, freezing, or canning the overflow. But when winter comes, that hard work means a store of food lasting through winter.

In July, I will awaken one night when the windows are wide open, and hear a chattering, a high pitched squeal, the sound of a raccoon mother calling her babies closer to her. The first time I heard the noise, I crawled quietly downstairs and shone a flash light beam out through the screens into the darkness. The raccoon family was so surprised they all scampered up a tree in the front yard and when dawn came, I went outside to see babies hanging from the tallest branches like ornaments on a Christmas The mother waited patiently on a lower branch for them to descend.

Then August comes, bringing hot scorching days and hot sultry nights. One evening, I hear the crickets singing. I always wonder of they were singing the night before. Autumn is just around the corner.

I will be watching for the squash and watermelons to ripen now. We are beginning to yearn for fall and the cooler days, cooler nights, having adjusted to the fleeting nature of the season, turning our thoughts towards the next one. Its inevitability softened by wanting it to come.

The four seasons of Wisconsin life lay their claim on its residents. We begin to feel that our yearning for the next season is as much a part of the changeover as natural forces. So we turn our hearts to the next season before its time so that it will come, as it is supposed to. We would be disappointed in an endless season of summer, although only three months ago we wanted nothing more than that summer should last forever. Now it is autumn's turn. Our hearts have been aligned with the movement of the earth on its axis.

Chapter Twelve
Country Picnic

My father invited Eloise to Joe and Jean's annual 4th of July Landowners Appreciation Picnic, a lavish affair with tables of food. On the day of the picnic, he announced that she would not be attending.

"Is she sick?" I asked.

"No."

"Something come up so she can't make it?"

"Nope," he answered.

"Did Eloise…" I began.

He interrupted. "Let's not go into it, please. Eloise and I have parted ways."

"Why?"

My father looked at me, exasperation written on his face.

"I suppose if I don't tell you, you'll hound me to death. Can't I have any secrets? Eloise told me that she didn't see a future for us. Heck, all I wanted was a good time. I wasn't looking for a long term relationship."

"Well, maybe you'll meet someone else," I said brightly.

"That's right. And there aren't many men as good looking as me either. So let's get a move on so we can get to the picnic where I'll scout the ladies."

We had to park half a mile away and hike the blacktop road to Joe's farm. Cars lined the right of way, and by the time we arrived, I was wet with perspiration. Unlike my father, I hated events like this. He dragged me to the picnic last year, and then abandoned me.

I took consolation in the food being plentiful and homemade. Ice cold beer. Gallons of lemonade made from real lemons, and sweetened with honey from a neighbor's aviary. A succulent roast pig.

There were dozens of different kinds of summer salads. Jean's potato salad is the epitome of perfect—red potatoes, hard-boiled eggs, mustard, and sweet pickle relish, the first of the garden onions, all mixed with a generous portion of mayonnaise. Other salads— coleslaw, green tossed salad, fruit salad, Jell-O salads—fill in the spaces between the roast pig and potato salad.

The Jell-O salads sparkled like a rainbow on the long food table. Lemon with celery and green peppers, orange with mandarins, lime with pineapple and cottage cheese, red with canned sweet cherries, and blue with blueberries and cream cheese layered together. You could fill your plate with Jell-O, and go back for more.

Green salad is my favorite and Jean makes it the way I like, romaine, red leaf, and green leaf lettuce tossed with thin slices of red, yellow, orange, and green peppers; celery chopped into crunchy bits; shredded bright orange carrots; ripe juicy tomato slices, the first from the garden; pungent red onion; crumbled Feta cheese; toasted walnuts; crunchy croutons; and tangy Greek black and green olives. The salad dressings, blue cheese, French, Italian, and Thousand Island, all homemade, sat in tubs of ice.

Under the tall verdant shade trees, heavy green watermelons sat nestled in ice-filled galvanized washtubs. As the meal progressed, someone would carve slices of the deep pink melon, juicy and sweet with dark brown seeds lacing the pulp.

A row of picnic cakes sat on another long table. My favorite is a spice cake made from zucchini and frosted with creamy caramel frosting half an inch thick, though I could be tempted by the German chocolate cake with coconut, brown sugar and pecan frosting browned under a broiler; or the white layer cake with lemon filling and coconut frosting.

The food is so good you have to pace yourself. Most people stay all afternoon and into the evening. I hoped to leave right after we had finished eating but I probably wouldn't be able to talk my father into that.

One of Joe's employees had been waving to me all cropping season. Joe's tractors are big so it's hard to see into the cab. Most of Joe's employees are cousins or second cousins, and I'd met the pack of them at Joe's parties. But I didn't think it was one of them. So when a man looking like an aging wrestler, stocky build, medium height, blond hair that curled around his solid head came up to me, I had him pegged.

"Hello" he said.

"You've been waving at me," I replied.

"I didn't think you recognize me. My name's Alfred but call me Al," he said. "I farm over on Sunset Road. I help my mother out since my Dad died. I work for Joe in the spring and fall, after I've got my crops in. It brings in extra money."

Jean interrupted us. "The food is ready. Why don't you start?"

I looked for my father but he was in the center of a circle of folks. I pointed him out to Al. "You want some company while you eat?" I asked Al. "My father's too busy to eat right now."

"Sure, let's chow down some of that grub. "

Al and I sat at a small table under a tree. He had found it necessary to fill two big plates with food. We both dug in, eating in silence for a moment, enjoying the taste of the food.

He broke the silence. "You haven't told me anything about yourself. How come you're farming?"

I told him how I landed on the farm and that I planned to go back to school in the fall.

"You want to be a teacher?" he asked me incredulously.

"What's wrong with that?" I asked, feeling defensive.

" I used to be a teacher, but I left teaching when my father passed away. I took over the family farm. My mother is getting up in years so it looks like I'll be there for a while. Someone has to milk and put in crops for her. My brothers and sisters work at good paying jobs so none of them are going to farm."

"You're not married then?" I asked.

"Divorced. Three children, but they live with their mother."

"Don't you miss teaching?" I asked.

" I like farming a whole lot more than I liked teaching, but that's not saying much. Maybe someday I'll figure out what I want to be. Besides, this way I don't have to pay so much in child support."

I let that disclosure pass without commenting. It didn't speak much for him, I thought, nor did farming without real love for the land and animals. Obviously he didn't know what he wanted out of life.

The next morning I was drinking coffee in the dining room in my pajamas when I heard Joe's tractor pull in. The corn needed to be cultivated. One thing I liked about the way Joe ran his business was that he tried to rely on mechanical weed control instead of automatically spraying for the weeds. I heard the tractor idling by the back door and then a knock.

Al had told me yesterday that he thought I was pretty when he saw me outside. When I opened the door, Al was holding my straw hat.

"You forgot your hat," he said, handing me the hat I had worn to the picnic.

"Well thanks," I said.

Al didn't seem to notice that I wasn't dressed. He waited a second. "Would you be interested in going to the Lions Fun Fest next week?"

I quickly thought it over. I wasn't sure that I wanted to attend a social event in Rush River with him where everybody could see me. On the other hand, maybe some of the other single men would see me and get the idea that I was looking. I needed to somehow jump start my non-existent social life. I wasn't getting any exposure staying on the farm. Maybe Al was the answer.

On the day of the parade, Al picked me up. I had bought a new pair of shorts, and what I thought was a flattering top. Al didn't say anything about how I looked, though I caught a whiff of shaving lotion when he brushed past me to open the passenger side of the truck.

We dragged along the lawn chairs I had set out by the back door. We parked a block over from the main street, and Al carried the chairs. People lined the street, some already seated in their chairs, others standing. It looked like a good turn out.

The parade started shortly after eleven. The Lions Club was in charge of the parade. They had set up a stand in front of the bank where the president of the club and the parade judges sat. The Lions awarded prizes for the best floats. The stand was wired with sound, and we sat close enough to hear the announcements.

The color guard started off the parade. A hush fell over the crowd as the six veterans, most of them middle aged or older, marched down the center of the street. With their paunchy stomachs, I hoped they'd make it all the way to the end of the parade. They were sweating visibly, but they marched in step. I stood when the flag went by and placed my right hand over my heart. Out of the corner of my eye, I watched Al. He didn't remove his hat, as most of the men in the audience were doing.

It was an election year. Candidates for the state legislature walked up and down the crowd passing out literature. One of the candidates owned a fishing bait company. He passed out key chains with shiny metal spoons that looked like fishing lures. Next, employees from Bush Beans canning factory came down the line, offering short rolls of life savers that had been packaged to look like cans of baked beans.

The parade had horses and ponies, new and vintage cars, new and old tractors, and the current state representative riding his motorcycle. There were floats for the historical society, for the Girl Scouts, for the Boy Scouts, for the most popular bar in town that cooked broasted chicken and fish on Friday night. The tractor dealership had a float, and so did the chiropractor and local nursery school. Queens from the different summer festivals from small towns in the area rode on floats with their court of princesses, pretty girls wearing long ball gowns and tiaras in their hair. The county sheriff drove an antique car as his float.

The floats threw handfuls of candy to the children lining the sidewalk. Candy that didn't make it all the way lay in the street until children ran in bunches and picked up the suckers, bumble gum, and wrapped hard candy. When their hands were full, they ran to their mothers and dumped the loot in bags.

Ever so often, Al would get up and run out and pick up a piece or two for us. He grinned like a little kid. I giggled like an infatuated teenager. It seemed to be going well between us. For a while, I forgot about the list I had been building of his negative points.

At the village park, preparations for the chicken dinner had been underway since dawn. Lions Club members cooked, looking hot and sweaty. I spotted Fred, the auctioneer, hauling a load of chicken to the kitchen. The chicken was cooked down by the pond where the Lions had permanent cement block buildings for grilling chicken over charcoal. Fred drove a four-wheeler pulling a cart with big covered roasters of cooked chicken.

Fred pulled up beside Al and me, and idled the engine. "Well how's my favorite farmer doing?" he asked me. He turned to Al, "How'd you convince this good looking gal to go out with the likes of you?"

Al shrugged. He didn't say a word.

I picked up the slack. "Good turnout isn't it?"

"It's nice to see the community supporting us. Well, got to get this chicken over to the food stand. You going to the dance, Ruth?"

"Al and I will be there," I answered.

"Well Ruth," he said, "save a dance for me." He gunned the engine and took off with a jerk.

Al mumbled something under his breath that I didn't quite catch.

The featured event for the day was the antique tractor pull. The park was sprinkled with old tractors. Their fresh coats of paint in bright primary colors made the park seem even more festive.

As the old Oliver, Massey-Ferguson, International and John Deere tractors lined up, preparations on the track were underway. A tractor scooped dirt into a front loader and re-spread it, trying to level the long competition field. Men clustered around the tractors excitedly. Women gathered to gossip while the children whooped and hollered on nearby playground equipment.

Al and I strolled around, admiring the tractors. He explained what made each unique. I listened with apparent interest but what I wanted to do was sit under a shady tree and watch the crowd, eat chicken, and talk about anything but tractors.

When the line by the kitchen shortened, we bought dinners, and carried them to the beer tent to enjoy. We had barely started to eat when the pull threatened to start. Al gulped the rest of his dinner and told me he'd save me a spot. I was surprised to find myself alone.

My father was eating with a group. I could tell he was trying to make a move on a new woman, who seemed enthralled by all his attention. He noticed me alone and motioned for me to join them. I moved to his table.

When I finished eating, I dutifully went to join Al in the bleachers.

I am vigilant about ultraviolet rays and had slathered sun block on my body in the morning. I could smell flesh searing all around me. I fidgeted next to Al. My hair was wet from perspiration. My feet were swelling. I suggested we move to the tent and stand there to watch. Al glanced at me, "You go, if you want. I want to stay," he said.

He looked back at the tractors and seemed so engrossed that I decided to leave. I walked back to the beer tent where my father was still lounging. The woman had left. I asked him how he'd gotten along.

"All she wanted to do was talk about her grandchildren," he answered.

The point of a tractor pull is what the names says, for the tractor to pull the weight wagon down the dusty lane as far as it can. When the wheels spin, or the engine dies, the distance is measured. The tractor that pulls the weight wagon the longest length wins the cash purse.

A tractor pull moves slowly. I began to realize that Al found the competition more exciting than I. And as boring as the event was to me, I was beginning to find it more exciting than Al.

If you want action, a demolition derby is a better choice. Those souped up old clunkers roar and grind as they try to knock each other out of the competition. Antique tractor owners are a proud lot. They've restored and shined the bodies, rebuilt the engine, driven near and far for hard to find parts. The crowd, being center stage, that is the culmination of all their hard work and babying. They're not in a hurry to relinquish the attention.

Finally Al came to find me, looking red in the face and slightly melted. He glanced at his watch. "I need to head home for chores. I could stop back later at your place and pick you up for the dance when I'm done?" I nodded in agreement, though I lacked enthusiasm, but saw no way out of the dance. We walked to his truck. We had parked in shade but it had long since departed. The inside of the truck was like an oven. We rode in sultry silence to the farm. Al looking hot and weary watched me climb out.

"See you later," he called as he took off.

After I was cooled, I prepared for the dance, choosing a flirty skirt, skimpy top, sandals, and redid my hair and makeup.

I was hoping this would capture the attention of someone. Then I went back out on the porch with a sandwich and can of pop to wait.

Night was beginning to fall by the time Al pulled in. I had moved back into the house, away from the insects, and was washing a few dishes in the kitchen. I waited for him to come to the door. He hadn't talked with my father at the tractor pull and I thought he might want to say hello but he stayed in the truck. I grabbed my purse, and called good-bye to my father.

Al smiled at me as I climbed in, but once again he didn't compliment me. I mulled that over as we drove towards the dance. He and I talked, but our talk was scrappy, bits of talk about weather, chores, nothing that would weave us together.

The dance was well underway when we arrived. Like most community festivals, country western music is popular. The band wasn't bad, though too loud for talk. Couples younger than Al and I were dancing enthusiastically. We stood and watched from the sidelines, sipping beer. Occasionally we would see someone we knew and exchange a few words. Most of them came over to talk to me, while Al stood there, looking bored, not participating in the conversation. Off in the crowd, I watched Fred. He was there with a woman I didn't know. Fred and the woman were obviously having a good time. I had heard over the grapevine that Fred was getting a divorce.

Finally the band began sprinkling the sets with slow numbers, a fox trot, and a country waltz. I love to dance and had fantasized about how it would feel to have Al take me in his arms and move with me across the floor. I glanced over at him when they began another slow dance and raised my eyebrows in a question.

Al shook his head. "Sorry, I don't dance," he said. "Want another beer?"

I declined. Al left to get another tall one.

Suddenly Fred was there. "I won't take no for an answer," he said.

"I wasn't going to say no," I said.

Fred was a good dancer. He had rhythm and a strong lead. I hadn't danced a fox trot in many years, but it started coming back. I was getting into the swing when the song ended.

The band started playing a polka almost immediately.

I held up my hands to say no but Fred wouldn't listen. He pulled me out into the crowd, and showed me the step, and then we took off. I followed, and fell into the one, two, three rhythm almost immediately. Fred and I laughed as we danced. When the polka ended, I was panting.

"I'd love to take you for another spin, Ruth," Fred said, "but I have to get back to my date. I'll walk you back to Al. Have you gone out with Al before?" he asked.

"No, this is the first time,"

"Are you having a good time?"

"Not really," I answered.

"Well, I'm not surprised," he answered, but didn't elaborate.

We reached Al. He was drinking beer. When I joined him, he kept on drinking. For a fleeting moment, a sneer crossed Fred's face. But he suppressed it, and reached out to shake Al's hand. "Nice to see you, Al. You're with the prettiest gal in the crowd," he said jovially. "Hope you're enjoying her."

Al looked a little surprised. He shrugged and gave a half smile. Fred left me standing there. Neither Al nor I spoke. After awhile I said that I should probably go.

"I should too. Chores come pretty early. I need to get some sleep," Al said.

We walked to the truck. We drove in silence.

When we arrived at my back door, he leaned over, pecked me on the cheek, said, "Thanks," and reached past to open the door from the inside.

I stumbled out of the truck and he roared away, kicking up the gravel as he turned onto the driveway. The lights were off in the house, except for the light by the back door and the one over the kitchen sink. I looked at the clock on the wall in the kitchen. It was only eleven o'clock, but I didn't care. I was glad the day was over.

Chapter Thirteen
Going to Church with Charlie

One Saturday night, Charlie called. "Take me to church tomorrow," he commanded.

"I usually don't go to church," I answered.

"I know," he said in his deep old voice, "that's why I'm calling. Bring your father along if you like. Pick me up at 8:30. I'll be waiting by the front door."

Click. The receiver went down. He had hung up.

So Charlie got his way.

I wasn't entirely surprised by Charlie's request. He had been mentioning that he'd like me to go to church with him for some time. This time he hadn't given me the opportunity to turn him down.

I hadn't been to church in so long I wasn't sure if women still dressed up. I settled on a skirt and blouse. My father wouldn't go, a lapsed Catholic, and not willing to shift his allegiance to a Lutheran Church.

Charlie was waiting, watching for my car. He made his way carefully across the sidewalk when he saw me drive up to the curb. He was wearing a dark suit. His hair was slicked down with oil. He was freshly shaven, and he carried a gray felt hat in his hand with a feather tucked in the hatband. I caught a whiff of Old Spice shaving lotion on his cheek as he pressed it to my lips for a kiss. He seemed like a different man. I had seen him only in overalls and work shirts until today. He made a commanding appearance.

As we drove, he gave me directions and told me about his church. "Not many folks go there anymore. Used to be a big congregation when my folks were alive, more than two hundred people belonged. Then someone got mad at the minister, and before you know it, most of them took off and built another church."

He pointed in the direction of a church on the edge of town. "But I stuck with my church. I was baptized there, and buried my parents in the cemetery out back. There's a place for me too between them. So I just keep going there and one day my body will rest there forever."

What can a person say after words like that?

I followed the road he had directed me to take into the country. After a mile or two, I could see the white steeple sticking up over the farm fields. The church sat back from the road, next to a big white house about five hundred feet away. We pulled up to the church and I parked next to a few cars already in the small parking lot.

It was one of those white wooden country churches you see in paintings of the Middle West. The front stained glass windows were symmetrical, one on each side of the double front door. In the middle, a set of concrete steps with wrought iron hand railings on each side led up to the door. The lawn was mowed, and on each side of the steps there were plantings of white spirea and the bright red geraniums. The white blossoms were past their peak and the round petals looked like confetti against the black dirt. I could see the minister, an old man himself, standing in the vestibule wearing a black robe with velvet collar. His gray hair was cut short. He was a tall thin man, who looked like Abraham Lincoln.

Charlie got out of the car and carefully placed his hat on his head. Charlie and I made it up the steps slowly. The minister was beaming at me. "Charlie told me he was going to bring you one of these Sundays. I'm happy to see that you've joined us. And it's a beautiful Sunday to celebrate the words of the Lord, don't you think?" He waved his hands in the direction of the fields that surrounded the old church. The corn marched up and down in neat rows as far as my eyes could see.

Charlie and I slowly shuffled through the vestibule in the church. We stopped and he caught his breath. Now he led the way. We walked down the center aisle past simple oak pews to the third pew on the right. Then he motioned for me to go in. I was headed for the end of the pew but he stopped me halfway down.

"This here's my spot," he said. He dropped his body down to the wooden pew. I sat down next to him.

Members beamed smiles in my direction. Four older women, their gray hair in tight sausage curls, sat in one pew, and a younger woman and two children sat behind them. After awhile, a couple made their way into the church, and sat in front of Charlie and me. They turned around and we exchanged pleasantries. A man and woman sat on the first pew on the right. A few more drifted in, mostly older folks. The congregation sat there visiting quietly, waiting for the minister.

Then a woman made her way to the organ. She straightened her music, and sat there gazing out over the congregation as she watched the back door, her spine straight as a lightning rod. Finally, she put her hands down on the keys, and started playing the opening processional. The minister came down the aisle, walking briskly, his robes flapping around him, and made his way up to the lectern on the left.

We followed the service in our bulletins, singing, reading responsively, and reciting the prayers when indicated. Finally, one of the women sitting with the group of four crawled over her neighbors to make her way to the front to sing a solo. The song was "Amazing Grace."

The singing of hymns made lack of members apparent. Most of us could not sing, but we all valiantly tried to carry a tune. The organist made up for lack of voice and quality by playing extra loud. As it turned out, Charlie had a wonderful voice. His baritone rang out melodiously over the others squeaking and squawking their way through hymns.

The minister began his sermon. He preached about love, how it is hard work to love those who aren't lovable, and talked about Jesus and his love for lepers, paupers, and sinners. He preached enthusiastically, spitting in his excitement to make us followers of Christ's teaching. I found myself listening, thinking about his words. Charlie had his eyes closed but I didn't think he was sleeping. Then we made our way through one more hymn, and the minister walked to the back to say the benediction. The congregation seemed to rush out of the sanctuary.

"We go downstairs for cake and coffee," Charlie whispered in my ear as we got up to leave. So I followed him. After we had shaken hands with the minister, we took a set of steps downstairs. When we got down that set of steps, we stepped into a large room full of tables and chairs. The smell of fresh perked coffee was in the air, and in the window in front of the kitchen, a cake cut into generous pieces, plates, forks, cups, cream, sugar, and powdered creamer were set out. A pitcher of milk sat next to half a dozen glasses. Two ladies from the service were bustling around in the kitchen. The rest were already seated. So this is where everyone had rushed to after the service I thought to myself.

I helped Charlie dish up his cake, poured him some coffee and carried it to his place. Then I went back and served myself. By then the minister had changed out of his robe and joined us. He sat down next to me.

I was introduced to everyone in the room, though it was a mere formality. Everyone knew who I was and where I lived. We ate our cake, drank our coffee, and talked about why some of the other members of the congregation weren't there. I heard about Tim and Monica, who were out of town visiting their son who lived in San Diego. They'd be back next week. Mabel had taken ill and had called Florence this morning to tell her she wouldn't be coming to church. And Alfred hardly ever came to church.

When I heard the name Alfred, I could feel my eyes get big with the question. Was it the Alfred who had taken me to the Lions Fun Fest?

Charlie read my mind. He leaned over to whisper, "His name is Alfred Kuehnast and he's older than I am. He used to live on a farm on the other side of town. His wife died a few years ago and he stays with his daughter a lot of the time. He is going to be buried out back too, not too far from where I'll go."

Andrea, who lived next door and watched over the church, came and sat down beside us for a few minutes. She had two children. She had each one come meet me. Then they greeted Charlie with a big hug. Charlie gave each one a dollar bill. They thanked him politely. Andrea told me that he often gave them money when he saw them.

The minister was quite interested in finding out about my church history. I explained that I hadn't been a member of any church since high school and that I had been raised Catholic. "We can arrange to have you join the church if you want," the minister said.

Charlie answered for me. "Ruth wants to join this church."

I turned my head to tell Charlie that I didn't want to join, but before I could speak he put his hand down over mine, and squeezed it tightly. His hands had softened in the months he had been living in his apartment. I closed my mouth without saying anything.

The two ladies who seemed to have kitchen duty got up and started clearing away the plates. They took the dishes into the kitchen, put them into a dishwasher, and started cleaning up. One of the ladies brought over a wrapped piece of cake for Charlie to take home. They had put it on a paper plate and covered it with saran wrap.

"We know you like carrot cake," she told him.

"We're real lucky to have that dishwasher," Charlie told me. "Andrea comes over from her house on Sunday afternoon and makes sure it ran okay and puts the dishes away. It's real handy to have someone so close to the church. They own the farm this church sits on. Her grandfather helped build the church. He deeded the land over to the church when the church was built."

The minister asked one of the ladies when the next Ladies Aid meeting would be.

"Two weeks from Thursday," she replied.

"You might want to come to that," he said to me. "They plan who is going to bring the treats, vacuum, dust, keep the church looking nice. I'm sure they could find a job for you. I'll order you church envelopes," he continued. "Maybe they'll be here next week. I'll give you a call and come visit you at home. You can ask me any questions you may have about the church doctrine."

"Thank you," I answered.

Then everyone started pushing his or her chairs away. I glanced at my watch and saw that it was nearly 11 AM.

Charlie and I started up the steps. He hung onto my arm again, pulling himself up with the railing. When we made it out to the car, and he had gotten comfortable in his seat, he removed his hat.

He said, "See that wasn't so bad. It didn't hurt, did it?"

"No," I responded.

"Say, what kind of perfume are you wearing?" he asked.

"I'm not wearing perfume. I'm allergic to bees. I only wear scent in the winter."

His blue eyes twinkled like stars. "You're so sweet you smell like the best perfume from Paris."

Chapter Fourteen
Autumn Chores

In the fall, the vet comes to the farm to get the cattle ready for winter. My job is to herd them into the chute. Beef cows aren't nearly as domesticated as dairy cows. For the young ones, this may be their first experience with the annual routine. I have to do some fancy fast running, waving my arms like a windmill, before I can get them headed down the double row of gates that leads to my father who squeezes the cows with another gate so they will go into the cage.

Once in the cage, the only thing they can do to protest is kick. The vet stands on the heavy metal bars and sticks them with the vaccination gun. They holler and cry when the needle goes in, even though their hides are tough. Then my father twists their heads so that the vet can use a cutter to remove their horns. No one wants cattle around with horns anymore, except maybe on Long Horns where they are something of a novelty. My father daubs a special powder on to stop the bleeding and the other side of the cage is swung open so they can gallop to a holding pen until we've finished with the herd. Every year the job takes longer as our herd gets bigger.

Even though my job is not that hard, after a long day of that kind of work, it takes me awhile to recover. The more work I do on the farm, the more I realize that I have a body that is going to wear out someday. My back acts like it could give out now and then, my knees creak, and the middle knuckle on my right hand sometimes is swollen in the morning. Farming is hard work, much of it physical. In the beginning, it had been fun because of novelty, but the work was becoming routine while as physically demanding as ever. If my father had "a hitch in his get along", he never complained but I noticed that he got up slower from his chair nowadays, and went to bed earlier.

There is always work on a farm but a change in season seems to promise that the work will be less hard than the season before. In autumn, the wise farmer considers the ant, as the Bible suggests, readying for a hard winter while hoping it will be mild.

Although there is no true season of rest on a farm, beginning with autumn and continuing into winter, longer nights make it possible for rest and sleep to soothe and mend the aching body without worrying about wasting daylight.

When the birds depart, a lonely feeling descends over the farm. The absence of songbirds makes the farm quiet. Barn swallows linger after the songbirds leave, but then they migrate south. Now, there are only a few species of birds left. Goldfinches and English Sparrows will remain here. The goldfinches will lose their bright yellow coloring as winter draws closer. Bluebirds are still here as well, and their sweet sound, normally drowned out by the noisy robins and blackbirds, fills the trees.

I like this time with the bluebirds. The juncos and chickadees have not yet moved south from Canada. The bluebirds will stay until late October.

I keep the birdbath filled with clean water. Before they depart, they will swarm to the birdbath to bathe and clean their feathers, flapping their wings, churning the water like a tidal pool as they wash. Their little bottoms gyrate as they swish their feathers around in the pool. Then they fly up to the corncrib roof to dry. The next day I awake to discover them gone.

Earlier in the spring, I happened upon a fledgling bluebird under the locust trees in the front yard right before I was about to mow. I ran inside for my camera and lay on my belly in the grass while I snapped photos. I was zooming in closer and closer, getting better and better shots, when the mother bird began diving at me like a bombardier. When I had a good photo, I retreated before she made contact with my skull as she threatened to do. Later, I went out to check if the fledging had flown away, and it was gone. That baby was probably one of the birds bathing in the birdbath this fall.

Harvesting the field crops and the last vegetables from the garden, this is urgent work as we move closer to winter and harder frosts. Pumpkins, squash and decorative gourds lie like bright balls in the midst of dying vines. Apples hang ripe and heavy from boughs.

We must clean out the root cellar. Soon we will lay in our stores of potatoes, apples and squash. A dry dark cool part of the basement is reserved for the bags of onions so that they will not sprout.

The potato crop comes in first. We've been eating potatoes since mid-July when the first red ones take on some size. Red potatoes are thin skinned and moister than baking potatoes, perfect for steaming or boiling, and wonderful scrubbed and fried in oil until the flesh is soft and tender and the outside coated with a crispy edge. The earliest reds can simply be scrubbed clean, no need to peel. The red potatoes won't hold as long in storage, so we eat them first. Eventually all the potatoes must be dug. Now I remember why I keep the potatoes weeded all season. Once the plant has died back, it is hard to find the hills under a tangle of weeds.

Kennebec, a light tan oval tuber, is an excellent all around potato because it bakes or boils equally well with its white, dry flesh, not to mention that its thin skin makes it easy to peel.

The best baking potato is a Russet, a long oval, deeper brown than Kennebec with a thicker peel and meaty white flesh. The peel is part of the taste experience when you bake them. The skin has been scrubbed clean, then buttered so they'll get crispy. Homegrown potatoes can be eaten down to the peel because they don't have the fungicides commercial growers apply to prevent mold and spoilage.

My favorite potato for mashing is Yukon Gold, a buttery yellow, wonderful mashed with their creamy-yellow flesh and rich hearty flavor.

With all the varieties of garden potatoes, peeling is not a chore. The act is another form of meditation, a gift of living off the land. Each potato presents a challenge, to peel it cleanly, exactly, without waste. Though we will fight potato bugs on the plants with chemicals if we have to, the potatoes themselves are free of chemicals. When I go to the grocery store, I take notice of the cheap potato prices. I sometimes wonder why I take on the work of a potato patch. But when I taste the fruits of our harvest, nothing, except a garden tomato, tastes as good, especially now that few things are growing in the garden. Our potatoes will last all winter under proper storage, and any left in the spring will be used to grow next year's crop.

With some urgency, the next job is bringing in the winter supply of wood. Our wood for this winter is already cut and seasoned, lying in a jumble of neatly cut lengths under the hardwood trees. A sawbuck sits in the middle of the jumble. This wood was cut last winter, when snow lay everywhere. Now we can bring it in; its rest outdoors under the trees has seasoned it. It is now dry so that it will burn clean without leaving creosote on the chimney walls.

We throw it into the pick-up, riding back to the house, truck springs groaning under the weight of the wood, sun shining though the branches half-dressed in their colors, as we make the bumpy trip back home, drinking in the blue skies, warm sunshine, storing the memory until next year.

Then we throw the wood out of the truck, peeling off another layer of clothing as we work up a sweat. Then the splitting maul is located in some back corner of the tool shed, spider webs brushed off with gloved hand, and my father sets to work to make the logs into firewood. I have tried, but I cannot lift and swing the maul hard enough to split the wood.

First he makes the oak pieces into big chunks. I imagine the feel of the fire on my hands when I come in frozen to the core to stand in front of the fire. I can see in my mind the color and look of oak when it has taken fire fully into its belly, a hot orange-red mass that retains its shape, emitting blue flames as its heart makes heat, and then becoming a lumpy mass of hot coals, glowing orange with yellow undertones, before finally dying down and sputtering out leaving only ash to tell of its glorious rise to hot fiery incendiary life.

My father splits some of the oak into kindling. A big pile of kindling by the fireplace is comforting. Crumpled newspaper burned first to warm the chimney, then crumpling more paper, laying a crisscross stratum of kindling, topping that with a few big logs. When touched by a match, fire will hungrily consume the stack.

As my father splits wood, I scurry around, throwing split wood into a pile by the basement window. We throw down enough wood to last all winter. The trip down and back up the steps will not be as bad as a trip out to the woodshed through snow and wind on a cold winter's night. If we need more wood, we can always fill a wheelbarrow and move it to the back door and carry loads to the fireplace. Usually we have it figured nearly right.

After it is thrown down the basement, then we descend the basement steps to pile the wood into neat rows. It seems there is never an end to the work wood brings. The night after making wood I sleep the sleep of the dead. No matter that I arise with some of my muscles protesting. As I lay my head on the pillow, the feel of the soft bed under me is all I need to make the transition into blissful sleep, awakening with a start in the morning, unaware of the hours that have passed. That is yet another gift of the ritual of bringing in the wood—a deep delicious sleep seemingly without dreams.

The harvested squash and potatoes change the tone of our meals. Oven dinners start to take over, something I can make up ahead, chopping the squash into wedges to accept creamy butter, sweet brown sugar, a little salt and pepper, making a meat loaf with the garden onion chopped into fine flavorful bits, and potatoes scrubbed clean of dirt so that they can be eaten down to the skins.

Or I take out the old blue enamel roaster, the one with years of pot roast burned onto the surface as a patina. I put the roast in, with two or three bay leaves, onions, potatoes scrubbed and quartered, probably red ones while they last, Kennebec when the reds have run out, carrots cleaned with a brush and quartered and shortened to lay between the cracks, maybe a little celery overall, seasoning of salt and pepper, a few garlic cloves nestled in the tiny spaces between the roast and the vegetables, and the meal slowly cooks while we are outside working up a hunger.

Later I'll add to the oven dinner, maybe an apple crisp, or baked apples topped with a dab of sweet butter, a generous pinch of brown sugar, maybe some raisins. When we walk indoors after hard work out in the open air, the smells are those of a rich, layered, mouth-watering mixture of meat, vegetables, and fruit, a meal that no fine restaurant can come close to matching when hunger is sharp and present. Hunger, real hunger, makes any meal a gourmet meal.

The shapes and colors of the fall harvest are big and tangible. Squash comes in different colors and shapes. Spaghetti squash has yellow skin, its shape long and cylindrical, almost like a watermelon. Hubbard squash has a warty dark green exterior, its big belly tapering off at both ends to short stubby ends. Turks Turban is a mixture of green and orange and white, like a wild stirring of paint in those colors.

Acorn squash has neat ridges and green skin making it look like an oversized oak nut.

We hoist the squash from the ground, maybe sucking in our breath a bit from the heft of the Hubbard, and throw them into the wheelbarrow. There will be many trips up and down the basement steps to put the squash into winter storage.

Carrots can stay in the ground for a while. We dig some, which seem to grow sweeter and more orange with the colder days and nights, so that I can slice and blanch them for the freezer. Then, when I make soup, all I need to do is reach for the prepared carrots.

Finally, the carrots must be dug. Tugging and pulling, I start at one end of the row and as the long thick roots emerge, the soil seems to loosen so that the next carrot can be pulled a little easier. I rinse the carrots with the garden hose, and dry them in the sun. Then I put them into pails and take them down to the basement where I cover them with sand so that they will not grow and lose their sweetness in the darkness of the cellar.

Carrots are good eaten raw and good cooked. When I cook them, I slice them thinly and simmer them gently with a pinch of sugar to bring out their flavor even more. Shredded, carrots make flavorful cakes with raisins and nuts and cream cheese frosting. Carrot bread and carrot muffins are also treats. Carrots go well with the sweet spicy taste of clove, cinnamon, nutmeg and ginger. The smell of a baked carrot cake resembles the cargo of a sailing vessel from the Far East returning to port with its store of spices.

The fall harvest takes away some of my sadness that the more tender vegetables have given way to frost. The green beans, peas, zucchini, radishes, and lettuce are long gone. Now it's cabbage, tender and crisp, replacing those vegetables. Cabbage can be diced for cole slaw, chopped for soups, sliced and sautéed in butter. Excess cabbage can be made into sauerkraut.

Tomatoes are gone too, though I usually have a store of them down the basement, wrapped individually in newspaper when the green tomatoes have run out of time to ripen. I keep watching for them to ripen, and when they are ready, bring them up to add bright color to a plate of yellow, white, and green.

Now that days are shortening, fall gives us back evenings inside the house. Too dark, often too cold, there is nothing to do but go to the easy chair and rest a spell after the evening meal has been eaten. The dishes are washed, draining in the rack; counters wiped clean of splatter and crumbs.

As I sit in my chair in a corner of the living room, a clock ticks steadily from some back corner of the house. I rattle my newspaper, reading about events in the world, feeling like I am on an island in space so far removed from trouble and turmoil. I let the foot rest up, push back, and relax. I pet the cat. The dark quiet world outside has gone to sleep and soon I too can go to sleep, but for now, I simply relax, breath deeply.

After crops have matured, after frost has come, there is a period of time when farmers breathe a sigh of relief. It's too early to harvest. For about a month, we are free from worry. Then, we start watching for the combine.

I know Joe does his best to harvest on time, but we are usually at the end of the line. Once the soybeans are ready, I worry about an early snow until the soybeans are off the field. Once soybeans are harvested, I worry less.

Corn can stand all winter if need be; a snowstorm isn't nearly as fatal on corn, although the longer corn stands, the more losses there are. Weather and animals take a bite. But the corn has never had to stand all winter. Joe comes with his big machines and in one day, the field is shorn.

Late autumn and winter bring that peace of mind that comes from having survived another cropping season. We always hope for a bumper crop, but we always settle for what Mother Nature will give us. Year after year we go through this cycle, worrying our way through crop planting, growth, maturation, and harvest, and year after year, we breathe a big sigh when the season is complete.

The last thing Joe does is ready the fields for the coming spring. Hopefully he manages to disk in the corn and beanstalks, maybe do some deep tillage in the wet spots.

I love the look of the fields when the season permits that final step. We are one step ahead of spring. The land looks neater, bedded down for winter this way.

The first snow around Thanksgiving will lie in the furrows and the fields will be striped brown and white until the snow melts. Usually the first snow melts. When the snow stays, and more snows begin building blankets of snow, autumn is gone, though this may be several weeks before winter solstice officially arrives.

Asian Beetles join us inside. They find the smallest entrance and seek shelter where it is warm. The beetles fly around the house on a sunny day, some giving up before spring allows them to make their escape outside, lying dead on tabletops and floors. The first year, I would lovingly take a found beetle to the door or window and release it to the outdoors, feeling like Albert Schweitzer who wouldn't kill any living thing. Hundreds of beetles later, I have lost my reverence and respect for the life of Asian Beetles. Now I hunt with my vacuum cleaner, sucking them into the bag, running the nozzle along the ceiling, around the windows, behind the curtains, where they cling. It has become a war, but in the end, I will lose.

All winter long, I come upon beetles, especially in the kitchen, where they dance around the overhead fluorescent light fixture as their last living act, and then fall dead to the floor. Polka dots of dead hope litter our home until spring, and then one day all the remaining live ones fly out the cracks to the great outdoors and resume their destiny of consuming aphids.

My father has worked hard all spring and summer. Many of the autumn chores fall on his shoulder—splitting wood, hauling baskets of produce down to the root cellar, making one last cutting of hay for the big round bales he has stockpiled for the beef cattle—but as the season progresses, there is less and less for him to do. He begins working indoors. One of his projects was to turn an old shed into a wood working shop. He insulated, finished the inside, and installed electricity.

We have become so used to working that leisure is no longer watching TV. Now we are engaged in activity that relaxes by engaging our other senses. For my father, it is building birdhouses and installing them wherever he can find a home. By word of mouth, he finds homes for the bluebird houses he makes in his shop. He also makes houses for wood ducks. If someone promises to maintain the birdhouse, my father will build and install it free. He says he wants to be like Johnny Apple Seed, and leave behind a legacy that will outlive him.

Quilting becomes my new hobby. After I joined Charlie's church, I learned that there was also a quilting circle that met once a month. I started going, and before long I was addicted. The ladies in the church were more than happy to teach me how to quilt. I acquired a stash of fabric, purchased a new sewing machine, and set up a sewing room in one of the bedrooms upstairs.

Until I became a farmer, I used to think Thanksgiving was a bit late on the calendar. After all, the kitchen garden had long since expired. But on a farm, Thanksgiving is timed perfectly. The harvest on the farm is usually done by Thanksgiving, and we give thanks for that. I love the Thanksgiving feast. Our table groans from the food, most of it grown right here on this land. The menu consists of mounds of fluffy mashed potatoes, sweet corn cut off and frozen, Hubbard squash, frozen green beans baked with cream of mushroom soup and French fried onions, sweet potatoes baked in their skins, and squash and pumpkin pie. The relish tray has pickles, sour and sweet, that I have canned as well as zucchini relish, pickled green beans with dill and hot peppers, and corn relish.

The self-sufficiency of providing so much of our own food is a source of pride. This is a tangible contribution; this is what I was seeking when I made the leap to farming.

As autumn deepens, I spend less and less time doing farm chores. Now I am sitting in the dining room surrounded by schoolbooks to read, prepare for exams, and write term papers. Although it had been more than a decade since I graduated from college the first time, I find that I am a better student this time around. My father tells me he thinks I'll be as good at teaching as my mother. As I bend over my schoolbooks, I remember how she looked bending over the stacks of papers she corrected at home while she supervised our homework. I now realize how dedicated she was to teaching.

Even Charlie has noticed that I am busy and involved with other things. He called me up one night. "I haven't seen you in weeks. When are you coming to visit me?" he asks.

"Maybe this weekend, Charlie. Right now I'm working on a term paper that is due on Friday."

"You like school as much as you thought you would?" he asks me.

"It's not school I like so much. It's where it's going to take me," I answered.

"That's the kind of answer I like to hear," he answered. "Just think, when you left California, you had no idea you'd become both a good farmer and a good teacher."

"Well, I'm not a teacher yet," I said.

"But you will be, sooner than you know it."

"I'll be over on Saturday, Charlie."

"Okay, I'll have the coffee pot on," he answered.

When I hung up the phone, I let Charlie's praise wash over me for a few seconds before I returned to my work. That was the most praise he had given about my becoming a farmer, and if I knew Charlie, he wouldn't repeat himself. The scarcity of the words seemed to make them sweeter.

Chapter Fifteen
Winter

On a sunny winter day, the inside of the house is especially cozy and inviting. I love to sit in the dining room when the sun pools on the table. I bring homework and a cup of hot steaming coffee to the table, and feel the pleasant room sparkling around me like a diamond necklace as I drink in the sun through all the pores of my body.

On such a day, there is a short luminous period just before the sun falls below the horizon. The world looks magical, as if surrounded by a glass bubble, as if the world is inside a snow globe. The lines of buildings are sharp and distinct against the horizon, trees starkly etched.   I feel a sense of pausing. The horizon is bathed in pinks and yellows, softened by darkening sky. I feel peace descend as night takes over from day.

Just after the sun has fallen below the horizon, I like to look at the line of trees on the west. Their trunks and branches are outlined against the remaining light in the sky. There is a clean simplicity to the silhouettes as the sun dips down in the sky.

My father and I burrow into our nest in winter. We have nothing to do outside except care for the cattle, shovel snow and watch winter birds at the feeder. That's what we tell ourselves, although at the end of the day, I realize that nothing to do keeps me busy all day long. I'm just like the birds, always moving and active.

Juncos and chickadees are active feeders. Juncos hunt for seeds on the ground, their small, dark gray bodies standing out clearly on the snow. Chickadees visit the feeders, flying around so energetically one wants to get out there and join them in the fun of eating seed.

We hang suet baskets underneath the Norway spruce. Downy and hairy woodpeckers come to eat, hanging upside down, or traveling up and down tree trunks, the bit of red on their small black and white bodies bringing Christmas color to the yard. House finches and gold finches have changed to drab gray, but their presence still cheers me. We have blue jays too, and their blue against spruce green and white is beautiful. An occasional spot of red helps me find cardinals.

Winter is when we plan the next year. We decide on crops, purchase seed, prepare taxes, and attend farm seminars. We order tree seedlings from the extension service to be planted in some corner of the farm in April. We dream of the coming seasons when activity is high, but rest during this season of seemingly nothing much to do.

I am working part-time at the credit union between classes at the university in Clear Water, making progress towards my dream. My father does what he can to help with the household chores, concocting a batch of chili, or a pot roast simmering slowly in the old electric cooker.   We eat as soon as I get home, and clean up the dishes together, leaving behind a shining clean, orderly room when we turn out the light to go to our chairs in the living room. Later, close to bedtime, one of us will pop a batch of baby rice white popcorn, small tender kernels full of flavor, coated with melted butter, before we turn into our beds for a winter sleep.

I will have the long slow evening to enjoy. Maybe that's the best part of winter, the long slow evening. It seems like it stretches out like the country roads I like to walk, long, undisturbed, untroubled. We'll be planning the garden then. Seed catalogs start arriving in December, and reach a flood by January. We go through each one, spotting a variety of a vegetable we haven't tried, or finding vegetables we've never grown.

Every new garden year is an opportunity to try something new. We keep the pile of catalogs by our chairs. Any thoughts of downsizing the garden that I had back in late summer when I was staggering under the load of vegetables that needed processing have been forgotten. Downsizing a garden is impossible when snow is one the ground.

By January, we've sent in our order. The die has been cast, and the garden will be as big, or bigger than the year before. The seeds arrive in trickles from the different companies.   I arrange them in my seed box, rubber banding together the packets by when they go in the ground. I have a large assortment of seeds. Using up seed is almost impossible; unless it's something I grow long rows of. I hesitate to discard seed. I hang onto packets until my box is so crowded, I must thin them like vegetables planted too close together.

Our chairs are cozy and warm beside the fire. We keep a fire going constantly. Stoking the fire gives my father something to do. He brings the wood up from the basement and piles it in the wood box. Sometimes I have to fight with my cats to get to my chair. They will move from them reluctantly, leaving behind the soft downy fur of their underbellies. I keep two cat beds near the fireplace for them. Sometimes, my father and I take a nap, with two cats at our feet also sleeping. When I am awakened by the sound of someone's snores, I am never sure if it is my father, the cats, or I.

Snow has other benefits besides giving us something to use for recreation when we are through with shoveling and chores. Animals write on the snow, telling stories about their activities.   After a fresh snow, I can see clear prints of their feet, and their usual routes. I often look out my bedroom window just before crawling into bed at the winter landscape swept by moonbeams that shows the snowy fields and nothing else. But in the morning, when I walk across the field, I see an array of tracks. Most common are the white tailed deer. I know deer live in the woods, but I am surprised at how close they come to our house. Their heart-shaped pointed tracks are everywhere. As I walk farm roads, it is very clear to me that there are deer highways out there. Clear paths mark the route.

Sometimes I walk across the fields to examine the prints. I am not a very good tracker, but I know there are coyotes, wolves, and red foxes living all around us. I've seen the red fox a couple of times, but it is an active nocturnal creature in the east eighty where the spring bubbles up and forms a small creek before disappearing again. Raccoons, skunks, opossum, rabbits, porcupine, rats, squirrels, and deer mice are all common. I used to think my father and I were all alone out on our farm. I now see that we are far out-numbered by other creatures. Just because we can't see them, doesn't mean they aren't there. The evidence left behind on the snow is most convincing.

We both have cross-country skies and snow shoes. It's fun to strap them on, and take a walk or ski across the fields. One field has just enough slope that once we have cut in the trail, we can go back down and ski all the way down.

At night when I am in bed, I can hear the whine of snowmobiles. The two taverns in town are a watering hole for the snow mobile drivers and passengers. They do not cross our land, but they are near enough that I can hear the whine of the engine, like giant bumblebees.

During winter, the smell of acrid manure, not the sweet smell of manure in the barn, but manure ripening, rotting, and composting fills the air. Someone is cleaning their barn, applying waste to fields frozen solid. By spring, application begins in earnest, as manure pits are pumped empty. Big tankers make the rounds of dairy farms, pumping manure from open storage pits into tankers, and then the thick sludge is sprayed onto corn ground. The smell lingers for a day or two until finally dissipating. City folks complain about the smell but we are always on the look out for ways to get some for ourselves. Manure credits mean less money spent on nitrogen, but I have to be honest, the manure stinks when it's applied to someone else's land. When it's applied to ours, we call it liquid gold

We try to attend as many of the cooperative meetings as we can. The cooperative is a method of organizing many farm services. The cooperative was created in the state of Wisconsin. The power company, credit union, grain mill, dairies, creameries, farmer advocate organizations are organized as cooperatives. The annual meetings are designed to attract as many members as possible so that there is the needed quorum.   There is usually food served, door prizes drawn, and small token gifts like baseball caps, coin banks, calendars, pens, and bottle openers presented. Attending them requires the participants to first sit through the business portion, where officers are elected, by-laws amended or changed, and an annual review of the year given. The meetings are boring, but necessary. The agenda moves through the business briskly so that the group can eat. That's why everyone came, for the food and gifts. We go more to be seen, our attendance sending the message that we consider ourselves to be part of the community.

The dividends we receive at the end of the fiscal year are nice too, though one will certainly never get rich from cooperative patronage dividends. In a way they offset all the promotional check-off fees. The Dairy Council, the Beef Council, the Soybean Council, the Corn Council, they all take a small amount out of every check written to the farmer when the commodity is sold. One thing is sure about check-off fees; somewhere there is an office with workers receiving competitive wages, benefits, retirement, with job security, supported by the class of farmers who receive no benefits, competitive wages, nor benefits, including retirement. I don't know how this came to be, but two cents per bushel, or a few pennies per gallon of milk don't seem to rouse as much fire as low commodity prices. But now that corporate farms are replacing small farms, lawsuits have been filed in different states about the check-off fees, and some have been ruled unfair and have been terminated.

Christmas brings my brother and sisters and their families to the farm. There is something romantic about Christmas on the farm. The livestock lowing in the barn heating it with their body heat, real snow dusting pines, spruce and firs, smell of wood smoke, crackling of a wood fire, scent of a real Christmas tree in the living room, these are all part of expectations about Christmas that aren't necessarily experienced in the modern world. But we have them as part of our normal life, and the family flocks home to experience them and some of our peace and quiet also, I think.

My brother and sisters and their mates arrive looking tired and stressed, but when they leave, they look rejuvenated and relaxed. It is my father and I who are tired now, having cooked, and shepherded, and managed a holiday fragile with expectations. When they depart, we settle back into the days of seemingly nothing much to do, until the smell of spring begins to scent the air.

I will be leaving for nine weeks to do my internship in teaching. I will have to live away from the farm during that time. I will miss the farm, my father, and old Charlie while I am gone, but when I return I will be fully qualified to teach. I realize that next winter, everything will be different. I will be teaching, not enjoying the peaceful quiet season of life on a farm. No one disturbs us now, except for an occasional driver stuck in the snow looking for a tractor to pull him out. The snow falls deep and still, sometimes cutting us off from the outside world until the plow comes through, sheltering us with beauty and laying silence upon the fields like soft down-filled comforters.

Before I leave, I stop over at Charlie's, and bring several containers of his favorite cookies with me. I knock at his door. It takes a few minutes before I hear his heavy shuffle on the other side. When he opens the door, I know immediately that Charlie is not well.

"Oh Charlie," I cry, "you're sick."

He was already shuffling back to his chair. "Well, come in then and stop letting the cold air in the door." he responded gruffly.

I followed him to his chair. I reached over and felt his forehead for signs that he had a fever. He pushed me aside roughly.

"Dog gonnit. Leave me be," he said. I recoiled from his harsh words but reminded myself that he did not feel well and probably had a right to his crabbiness.

"Have you seen a doctor," I asked quietly.

"My brother took me yesterday. They want me to go to the nursing home awhile so I can be looked after by a nurse."

"What did you tell them," I asked.

"Well what do you think I told them? The last thing I want to do is go to a nursing home. I'm not going to live much longer, and I don't want to spend one more day in one of them places than I have to, I can tell you that much."

Inside I secretly smiled. Even though he wasn't feeling well, he was still Charlie.

"Well, I don't blame you Charlie. But you need someone to look after you. Darn, if I weren't going away so soon, I would come and take care of you. But I have to leave the day after tomorrow."

"Well, look after me until you go. Then I'll go to the home if I have to," Charlie finally said. He reached for my hand. "Ruthie, I'm not afraid to die. What I am afraid of is taking too long to die."

"You're not going to die yet, Charlie," I said. "You're…" Charlie interrupted me.

"Let's talk about something else besides my health. Show me what you got inside them containers."

I opened up one and showed him the cookies. I had made molasses cookies and sugared their tops and stuck a raisin in the middle just like Charlie's stories of his mother's cookies. He reached in for one of the cookies. His hand shook but he managed to grasp one and bring it to his mouth.

"Mmmm, mighty good," he said. "Could you go down to the kitchen and get me some milk?"

"Sure Charlie, whatever you want."

When I got back, Charlie had straightened his shirt out and combed his hair. I sat down on the coach and we talked for a while.

He interrupted me. "Why don't you go out to the video store and bring back one of your favorite movies and we'll watch it together." He pointed to a player sitting under the TV. "My brother brought over one of them machines the other day so I'd have something to do now that I'm starting to go downhill."

I overcame my surprise. "Do you have a favorite movie?" I asked Charlie.

"Not really. I like the ones with cowboys and pretty girls in them. Do you think you could find me one of them?"

"I could probably find you several," I said.

"And while you're at it, bring back a pizza and some pop. We'll have an evening right here together."

So that's what I did. Charlie dozed off in his chair ever so often but he'd always pull himself back to the movie in a few minutes. At the end of the evening, he asked me to come back the next day.

"This time bring me some Chinese food," he said. His blue eyes could still sparkle now and then. They were twinkling back at me. "And see if you can find that movie 'Casablanca' with Humphrey Bogart and Ingrid Bergmann in it," he said.

But after that day, I really had to leave. I had stayed up late both nights to finish my packing so that I could spend every waking moment with Charlie. I waited as long as I could but I knew I had to say good-bye. Charlie seemed to sense my worry.

He brightened up and said, "I believe I feel better after these last few days. I'll be waiting right here for you to return. Now you better get home so you can get up early and get a good start on your drive."

I started to tell him how much I hated to leave him, but he shut me up. "I want you to go. I wouldn't want you to stay behind because of me. I'm an old man at the end of my life. You're just beginning yours. Now go on and get."

"Won't you let me hug and kiss you," I asked.

Charlie pulled himself out of the chair. "I don't know why you'd want to hug a dirty stinky old man, but go on, punish yourself." I put my arms around him and pulled him tight and gave him a big squeeze. Then I reached up and kissed him on his cheek.

His hand came around to my chin. He held my chin firmly and reached down and gave me a soft kiss on my lips. Tears were welling up in his eyes but I knew that I should pretend I hadn't seen them. "Go on now, get out of here," he said.

I reached for my coat and opened the door. When I turned around to say good bye one more time, he had turned his back to me so that I couldn't see his face. I shut the door quietly and put my coat on as I walked to my car. I could see him watching me from his window, peeking around the curtains like he didn't want me to see him, so I didn't wave. I put the key in the ignition and started the car, then pulled away from the curb. It was hard to do, but that's what Charlie wanted.

Chapter Sixteen

Saying Good Bye to a Friend

My father called me everyday while I was doing my internship. Charlie hadn't been able to stay alone more than a few weeks after I had left. His brother moved him to the nursing home in town. My father visited him almost every day. As the weeks passed, I worried that Charlie wouldn't last until I got home. My father said he was still eating, and getting more cranky and surly with each passing day, but was giving no indication that he was giving up.

My father tried to get Charlie to talk on the phone to me, but when he passed Charlie the phone, he would not take it in his hand. He would say, "I want to see her in person, none of that telephone talk. When she gets back, she can tell me all about her teaching experiences. Until then, she better be working hard. You tell her that for me, Arlan. Ruthie better be working hard."

Then my father would get on the line and tell me what Charlie had just said.

I missed Charlie as much as my father while I was gone. I loved to listen to Charlie's tales of growing up. He told me of adventure, of the old ways of farming, of the good and the bad.

He had loved to come eat with us, especially Sunday dinner. If it was warm enough, we'd sit outside on the front porch and Charlie would look around with interested eyes. Then, he would doze, and finally he would ask me to take him back to his apartment.

The last time he had come out, he had pointed out something in the shed where I parked my car. When we had looked at the farm, this was the only shed that had regularly received a coat of white paint. Charlie directed me to a back corner, three feet off the ground. I could barely make out what he wanted me to see. I had to kneel down and get close. I saw a heart carved into the timber, faded to gray now. The initials were B.T. and C.K. He stooped down as low as he could. The arthritis in his knees made it hard for him to get all the way down.

"My sweetheart," he said, "Bonnie Tollefson. But she wouldn't have me. She married my brother instead."

I felt a shock of recognition go through me. Charlie's brother took care of him, and did it well, but I had never seen Charlie's brother's wife with him. And Charlie's brother had never farmed. I had always wondered why only Charlie had farmed the land.

"It almost tore the family apart, but we patched it back together. But I swore I would never love another woman. I stayed loyal to the end. But," he said, "when you came along, I loved you like a daughter. If you had been around in my time, I would have fallen in love with you."

I put my arms around him, and gave him a hug and a kiss on his cheek.

On my last day of teaching, I received an anxious early morning call from my father. He had spent last evening sitting by Charlie's bedside. "It doesn't look good," he said.

"I'm packed and ready to go," I told him. "I'll be home before the sun sets on the farm. I'll go see Charlie immediately after I get home."

My students threw a party for me. They put a photograph of me standing in front of the class writing on the blackboard in the card, and all the students had signed it. I was touched by their show of feelings. I would show Charlie the card. Nine weeks away from the farm had seemed like eternity, and Charlie's illness had made me even more aware of the slow passage of time.

I had received permission to leave early so that I would get home before nightfall. I had explained about Charlie, about how he was sick and near the end of his life. Still, I looked forward to seeing everything in daylight as I drove over the last hill and entered Rush River. I wanted to see the village as I had the first time.

I came down the last hill before town around 4 PM. Because it was February, the sun was mid-point in the sky above the horizon and the shadows were warm and mellow against the snow. All around the village, you could see farms with their white houses and red barns dotting their plots of land. The land spread out wide like a small plain before it started undulating up to hills in the distance. At the bottom of the plain lay the village of Rush River.

The pond was still frozen although the creek feeding the pond was running free.   The town was quiet. School had been let out an hour ago so there were no crossing guards to slow traffic to fifteen miles per hour in the school zone. The restaurant by the pond was closed. It opened at six in the morning and stayed open through lunch. The village sign in front of the restaurant announced the winners of the children's ice fishing contest held every February. A small sign in front of the restaurant advertised "God Bless America!" on one line. Beneath it, the special of the day, "Spaghetti pie".

I drove through town slowly, drinking it all in, past the shops, past the library, past the service stations. As I approached the farm, my heart beat with excitement. The pine trees along the road were free of snow, but high snow piles that hadn't yet melted made the driveway hard to spot. I stopped at the entrance and looked up. Blue jays were taking their evening meal.   A cardinal flashed a bit of red color; I could see chickadees and juncos flying up and down like pepper blown down by the wind on ground too bland for spring.

I pulled onto the cement apron outside the garage. I had hardly gotten the car door opened when my father was there, hugging me like a bear, and asking me how I was. It felt good to be enveloped by his warm hug.

In the kitchen, I smelled pot roast in the old cooker. On the counter, a pan of peeled potatoes sat ready to be cooked for mashing. I looked around and felt the sweet rush from being home again.

Then I drove over to the nursing home to visit Charlie. I peeked in the door to see if he was awake but Charlie's eyes were closed. At first I couldn't tell if he was sleeping or resting. I sat in the chair by his bed and waited for him to wake up. I could hear the sound of supper trays rattling on the carts as they were distributed to patients in the infirmary. When they brought Charlie's tray, he opened his eyes and shook his head.

"Try to eat." the nurse asked. "You didn't eat breakfast or lunch, and nothing yesterday."

"Not hungry," Charlie said. "Take it away."

I pulled my chair closer, "How are you feeling Charlie?" I asked softly, patting his hand gently.

Charlie turned his blue eyes on me and shook his head. "Won't be long now. I'm glad you're back home. I wanted to say good bye."

I didn't understand at first, and then, sadness crept into my face. Charlie studied me a minute. "Don't go," he said. "Maybe it'll be tonight. I'm ready to go. Don't feel sad. I've had a good life."

I gave his hand a squeeze. I could see Charlie's eyes mist over and a tear drop form in the corner of his eye. He moved his head and looked at me. "Are you going to be a good teacher?"

"I love teaching," I answered. "as much as I like farming."

"Good," he said. " You'll have a good life. Remember when I'm gone; keep hold of what you love. Set your roots into that."

I leaned in to hear him better but he had finished speaking. Then he said, "Thank you."

I raised my eyebrows as if to say, "For what?" but he had shut his eyes. I could hear his breath change into shallow, quicker breaths, and knew he had fallen asleep. I sat beside his bed. The room became black with the shadows of night falling. I sat by his bed waiting.

There was a light knock on the door. I turned to see who it was. The doctor came in. He spoke in a loud voice, and Charlie's eyes jerked open. The doctor turned to me, "If I could ask you to step outside for a few minutes, I need to examine Charlie. When I'm done, you can come back in."

I got up to leave.

Charlie reached up to grab my hand. "Don't go," he pleaded. He held on tight.

I gave Charlie's hand a squeeze. "I'll be back soon," I said.

"Don't leave," he said to me, squeezing my hand tighter.

I repeated my promise to him. "I'll be back as soon as the doctor is done." He let my hand drop.

I went out to the hall and walked down to the family waiting room. I went to the phone and called my father. He didn't answer so I left a message and told him I wasn't sure when I would be home.

I hadn't noticed anyone in the waiting room, but when I turned around from making the phone call, I saw a man sitting in the corner of the room, reading a magazine. He looked up at me and smiled.

"How's Charlie doing?" he asked me.

"Not too good," I said. I had poured myself a cup of coffee and started sipping on the black murky liquid to hold back my tears.

"You've been awfully good to that old man," he said. He had gotten up from his chair and had moved across the room to talk to me. "Excuse me, I haven't introduced myself. I'm Jim Phillips. I live on the other side of Rush River. My mother is in the nursing home. I'm waiting for them to finish fixing her hair before I go see her. Then we'll go to evening chapel together.

He pointed to the sofa I was sitting on and asked, "May I join you?"

"Certainly," I said. He seemed to be a gentle, well-mannered man, graying at the temples, a little stooped in the shoulders, but energetic looking. I tried to think of what I knew of him.

"You raise dairy cows?" I asked tentatively.

"Used too. I sold the whole lot at auction last month. No money to be made. Too many long hours. I'm not sure what I'll do next. It's too early for me to retire. My wife died a few years ago. My children are in college now. It's a hard business when you don't have any help. It's time for me to try something else.   It was a good life, but it's not possible to live on a farm and keep it small. The family farm can't support you today. It's a place to live, but not a way of life. I'll keep a few animals.   Chickens because I like them. I like the gathering of eggs, the sound of the rooster in the morning, the cackle of the hens when I go into the hen house to harvest their eggs. I'm thinking about teaching. I have a degree in agriculture. I'll have to take some classes to get certified to teach but I wouldn't mind working in a classroom where I can do my work sitting down."

I felt myself relax in his company. I hadn't realized how tense I was while I sat by Charlie's bed. I started telling him about how I had just gotten my teaching credentials. Charlie's doctor interrupted us. I stood up quickly.

The doctor drew me aside. "He hasn't been eating the last couple of days. He told me he's ready to die. He's 87. He lived a good life. It's time for him to go. He's signed a living will and doesn't want life support measures used. It's just a matter of time. If you want to be there when he goes, you should probably stay the night. It could be tonight. It could be tomorrow or the next day. Charlie says it'll be tonight. The patient usually knows."

I called my father back to tell him what the doctor had told me, and to tell him to come when chores were done. Jim Phillips had slipped out of the room.

I went back into Charlie's room, and picked up his hand. I placed my lips on his hand and gave it a kiss. He smiled then, without opening his eyes, a soft gentle smile. I could feel his strength leave him. I sat down to wait some more.

When my father came later, I left them alone while I used the bathroom. When I returned, my father was standing there looking misty eyed.

Charlie said, "Go home now, Arlan," loud and clear. We were both startled. Charlie continued. "I want Ruthie to stay with me."

"I'm not going anywhere," I said, and sat down beside him. I put my hand on his, wrapping the old gnarly fingers that had spent their whole life working, with mine. I rubbed my finger gently across the back of his hand, feeling his old bones. He closed his eyes. I looked up to find that my father had slipped away.

Charlie seemed to be sleeping, but ever so often he would stir, agitated and frightened. I kept whispering to him that everything was okay.

Once it occurred to me that his brother might want to be here but when I whispered to Charlie, asking if he wanted me to call him, he shook his head. He strained to whisper, "Nothing more to say to him. We made it through life together despite our differences, but I am glad to be through with it. She didn't come," he said. "Right up to the end, she wanted no part of me. So be it," he said, and closed his eyes.

I must have drifted a sleep in my chair. I was awakened suddenly by Charlie crying out, "Momma, I'm coming home. Where's Papa? Is he here too?"

His breathing became more shallow. I leaned down to make sure he was breathing. I heard him take a breath in, and then he let it out slowly. His hand was burning hot, as if he was sending all his energy into my hand. I leaned closer to his mouth, listening for the sound of breathing. There was none. I sat there quietly. His color began to change and his hand was beginning to cool.

So this is how it ends, I thought, a breath, and then we slip to the other side. No drama, such a thin line between life and death. One breath, then the struggle is over.

I rose to tell the nurse.

Chapter Seventeen
The Journey Continues

Visitation for Charlie was held at the funeral parlor the night before his funeral. I had driven by the funeral home many times. On the corner, down a side street, in the middle of the houses that had been built when Rush River was being settled, it blended in with the old mansions. This neighborhood, with tall trees growing on the wide boulevards in front of the old houses with big front porches, made it seem like it was of a different world than the new subdivisions springing up around town. The porches of these homes had swings and white wicker furniture. If you didn't know the century, you would expect to see a team of horses pulling a buggy down the cobblestones. It seemed a fitting place for Charlie's friends to say their good byes.

Inside, the funeral home smelled of dust and old varnish. The floor creaked as the neighbors came to pay their respects. My father and I stood with the rest of the family. They had insisted that we do so, telling us that Charlie had thought of us as family.

It was here that I got my first look at the woman Charlie had loved but his brother had married. She was a tall angular woman, her long gray hair braided and wrapped around her head in an old--fashioned hairstyle. She was bony, thin as a string bean. When she smiled at me, her teeth gleamed pearly white and her whole face lighted up as if the sun had come out on a rainy day. Charlie's brother addressed her as "Mother" and didn't leave her side.

The line of mourners grew as the evening wore on. It seemed the whole town was coming out to say good-bye. I recognized many of the faces from the Credit Union. Around 8 PM, there was a late surge of mourners. These were older couples, smelling faintly of farm chores, looking weary from their day of labor, coming to see their old friend one more time.

The man I had met in the family waiting room also came to pay his respects. He was wearing a dark suit. I didn't recognize him at first. "Sorry for your loss," Jim Phillips said simply. He reminded me who he was. It seemed like a long time had passed but I had met him only the day before yesterday. We talked for a few minutes. When he left, he shook my hand once more, and said he hoped he'd see me again.

The funeral was held at the old church the next day at 11 AM. When we pulled up, I could see a mound of dirt by the freshly dug grave. Soon Charlie would be lying next to his parents. The thought made me feel happy and sad at the same time. He had planned for this day, just as he had planned for the next season of crops for more than sixty years.

The church sparkled inside. I knew that the ladies of the church had cleaned, scrubbed, and vacuumed; wanting the sanctuary to looks its best for Charlie's funeral. I noticed as I walked down the center aisle that the candle wax from the midnight candle service on Christmas Eve that had stained the rug for as long as I had been a member had been removed. I wondered who had bent down with a hot iron to melt it onto an old rag. Maybe Andrea, the youngest woman in the congregation, the one who could have dropped down easily to the rug and gotten up without a struggle. There was not a speck of dust, a stray cobweb, a piece of dirt anywhere in the church.

The place was packed with mourners, every pew filled just like it must have been in its early days. But the third pew on the right had been roped off. Charlie's hat had been placed on the pew, in the middle, its feather in the hatband looking as gay as ever.

The minister recited a long eulogy about Charlie, about how he had come to church every Sunday most of his life, joined in the fellowship, and then gone back to the farm to work hard for six more days, until the next day of rest came along. He mentioned me too, how Charlie and I had become friends in his last years on earth. I felt someone staring at me then and when I glanced in the direction of the eyes, I met the face of Bonnie, who blinked quickly and looked away.

As the tribute continued, I learned more about Charlie than he had ever told me. I learned how he had been a good neighbor to everyone in the community, helping out quietly, not wanting any recognition.

Afterwards, the family invited the mourners downstairs for the lunch.

The church ladies were serving the lunch. They had made sandwiches, and piled them on platters. There were bowls of Jell-O salads, hot casseroles of escalloped potatoes, baked beans, casseroles made with hamburger, potato and carrots layered with canned soup. The food was set out on the counter just like after church.

There were big stacks of plates and cups for the crowd. Desserts rested on the tables, platters of bars, and cakes, all homemade. I knew they had worked very hard to make the lunch special. They were trying to make a good impression on the visitors.

The room was filled with laughter. Voices rang out loudly as friends and neighbors caught up on news from the long winter. It took a long time for the crowd to start thinning.

I could see the ladies working hard in the kitchen. At one point, I attempted going into the kitchen to help with the dishes but they wouldn't hear of it. I could see the dishes stacked by the dishwasher that was already running and there were stacks of platters and pans by the sink to wash. They looked weary but determined not to let me help. I accepted their gesture as their way of saying they understood the loss I was feeling.

The minister came up to me to meet my father. As we talked, I realized how right Charlie had been to bring me to church. I was feeling a measure of comfort from seeing the pastor, hearing the platitudes about death that, though trite, were still comforting. Being in the church I had joined to make Charlie happy gave me comfort too. It had been such a small thing to do, but had meant so much to him.

The crowd was thinned now to mostly relatives. Bonnie came my way.

"Ruth, can I talk to you privately?" She was holding a brown paper sack.

"Sure," I said, but wondering what we had to talk about.

"Maybe we could go upstairs into the sanctuary where it will be private?" Bonnie started up the steps. I followed.

She walked into the sanctuary and sat down in a pew near the back. I noticed she had situated herself so that she could see the vestibule and anybody who might be passing through to the outside.

She pulled an old tattered photo album out of the bag. The front cover was half torn off and the holes in the pages had been ripped out, but the album was still intact.

"I took this from Charlie's apartment after we moved him to the nursing home. I went over one morning when my husband was visiting his brother. You have to promise you'll keep a secret. Will you?" She stopped talking and scanned my face. "You look confused, but I'll explain everything to you. But first you have to promise you won't tell a soul."

I wanted to say yes but at the same time, I felt loyal to old Charlie. She was the woman who had spurned him, turning his life into a lonely existence.

"I know I can trust you because Charlie did, but you have to swear that you won't reveal what I am about to tell you to anyone, not even your father."

"But why me?" I asked. "If it can't be told to anyone, why are you telling me?"

"I knew you'd ask that," she said. She pulled a letter out of the side pocket of her skirt. "Charlie sent me this letter before he died. In it he asked me to find the album to give to you to keep, or to throw away, whatever you wanted to do."

"May I see the letter?"

"There are some things in there I don't want you to read, but I'll show you parts of it." Then, she showed me Charlie's name at the end of the letter, the salutation, and a paragraph. Charlie was directing her to find the album and give it to me.

"I promise," I said quietly.

She handed me the album, then she pulled it back. "We better put it back in the sack so no one can see what it is. Now I'll explain what it's all about." She put it back into the sack and put the sack down next to me.

She took a deep breath and began. "I was Charlie's brother's girl from first grade all the way through tenth grade. Charlie was a year younger than his brother. I started going with Charlie in tenth grade. He was so cute and funny. I fell head over heels in love with him. But his brother was broken-hearted. He begged me to take him back. One night after a dance, it was a spring evening and a lovely night; he asked to walk me home. Charlie hadn't been able to go to the dance for some reason. I can't remember why exactly anymore. So I told his brother I'd meet up with him so that no one would see us leave together. When we met, he started in again, begging me to take him back. I felt so sorry for him. He cried and carried on so. Well, one thing led to another, and before we realized what was happening, we were hugging and kissing. We found a secluded spot away from prying eyes, and then, well, you know." She stopped talking.

I looked at her. She was waiting for me to say something. So, I asked her the question on my mind, "You had sex?"

"That's what happened all right," she said. "Of course, it would have been okay. No one would have known. I stayed broken up with his brother. The next day I wrote him a letter and told him that I really loved Charlie. Charlie and I carried on as if nothing had happened between his brother and me. But then, a few weeks later, I realized I was pregnant and the father could only be one man. To get myself out of the predicament I was in, I broke up with Charlie, and went back to his brother. No one ever knew for sure, though there was talk about it for years. Of course, by now it's all blown over."

She pointed to the paper sack. "In there are my letters to Charlie and some photos. There are photos of the family too, and the farm over the years. That's why he wanted you to have it, to preserve the history. I didn't remove anything, though I could have. I wanted you to know. I know you think I am heartless and mean. But all these years, I really loved Charlie. Of course, I came to love Raymond too. Now Charlie's gone and I've still got Raymond. I thought you should know the whole story. I don't know why. I guess I wanted someone to know a woman loved Charlie. You weren't the first. It's just that back then, it would have been a terrible scandal. Charlie and his brother would never have been able to patch it back together and one of them would have had to leave town. So, I fixed it the best way I could."

"I better slip out to my car and put this away," I finally said. As I got up to leave, I looked at Bonnie, sitting with her shoulders hunched over, looking miserable, and I felt a wave of sympathy. I sat back down and reached over to her and gave her a hug. "The secret is safe," I said. Then I got up and took the sack to the car.

Chapter Eighteen
More Changes

Charlie had been so much a part of our life on the farm that after he was gone from earth, I felt like a big hole had been cut out of my world. I needed his interest, his support, I discovered, after he was gone.   I had been his student, learning and practicing, under his watchful eye.

I saw him in every corner of the farm, riding his tractor, sitting on the porch, picking fruit from the orchard. Sometimes I would find myself setting aside a few cookies for him, or cutting an article out of the newspaper that covered a new way to farm.

Every time I got into my car, I saw the heart with his initials carved under Bonnie's.   I took solace that Charlie lived on in my memory and that Bonnie too held him deep in her heart but I couldn't shake my grief.

When I shared these feelings with my father, he didn't understand. I suppose he saw himself as holding first place in my heart. I know he too felt sad, but not in the way I did.

I was looking for a teaching job now. It didn't appear that I would get one in Rush River. The school system had a good reputation. When they had an opening, teachers with more experience applied. I was told that there weren't any openings for the coming school year, although they always needed substitute teachers. I considered doing that, but decided I had worked too hard. Anyway students were always harder on substitutes. I wanted a permanent position.

I was looking around the area, trying to find one that wouldn't require a long drive. Rush River was in the middle of a smattering of small towns, all rural. I had many choices. I set up interviews.

Each interview took me to a different school. Some of the schools were old and needed to be replaced. Other school districts had a new school complex set on the edge of town where all the grades were housed together. Each gave off some aspect of its character. Sometimes when I walked into the main office, I was ignored. Other places the staff looked up immediately, friendly and smiling. Administrators gave off their own aura, businesslike, compassionate, sloppy, or harried.

I had set the boundaries of my drive at about forty-five minutes. A state highway ran through Rush River, and connected with other state highways, which ran to these small towns. Three school districts had interviewed me so far, but none of them had presented an offer. None of them had felt quite right to me either, so I was continuing my search.

On this interview, I drove up to the school at mid-morning. The school wasn't new, but it wasn't old either. There were no students loitering just off school premises smoking cigarettes on a break between classes. I had seen that at one of the schools. As I walked in the double doors at the front, I could see the main office through big glass windows. There was a serene, efficient, orderly feel to the building as I made my way through the hall to the office. Posters and announcements were tacked up on a big bulletin board near the entrance. The trophy case was full of the students' accomplishments not only in sports but state forensics meets as well.

When I entered the office, a woman at the front desk immediately greeted me. "Here to interview?" she asked. "You must be Ruth." She gave me a friendly smile.

"Yes, with Dr. Garland," I answered.

"He's waiting for you." She gestured to his office, then suggested I hang my coat on the coat rack.

When I entered his office, he was working at his computer, but he immediately jumped up. "You must be Ruth Joseph," he began, "I've been looking forward to meeting with you." He grasped my hand firmly in a handshake, and smiled warmly. Then he gestured to a chair. I sat down in a chair across from the desk, but instead of him returning to his seat, he sat in the one next to me. He reached for some sheets of paper on his desk and handed me a copy.

Laid out on paper was the structure for the interview. I was to be interviewed by a team of teachers first, then the school board, and finally Dr. Garland. He said he would explain school policies and procedures and answer any questions.

"You are the last of eight applicants, so we will be making our decision shortly."

At the end of the interview process, I felt like I had done a good job answering their questions during the structured interview. I was impressed by the thoroughness and efficiency of the process. They were looking for an English teacher and for someone who would take over their Junior Achievement Club as well. They asked several questions about my business background in California.

I drove home, hoping they had liked me. I paid attention to the route, noting any possible short cuts, how the road would be in winter, those things. I stopped in the small town where the students lived, walking up and down Main Street, visiting some of the shops. I had a cup of coffee at the local restaurant and a piece of pie. I could see a strong Norwegian influence in the community.

When I got home, my father greeted me at the back door. "Dr. Garland called. He will be sending you an official offer in the mail tomorrow. He said to please call him if you have any questions. Congratulations!"

I grinned with pleasure.

My father gave me a big hug. "Now you can relax and enjoy the rest of your freedom until school starts."

Now that I was no longer preoccupied, I noticed that my father was beginning to show his age. Maybe he had been that way before; maybe my time away from him helped me see him more clearly. He never complained, but he wasn't getting up as early, and was going to bed sooner. Sometimes he lay down for a nap after lunch. His face looked more drawn, his shoulders more stooped. This was something new. I asked him to go to the doctor.

"I'll go, Ruthie, but the only thing wrong with me is time. I'm getting old."

Maybe if Charlie hadn't recently passed away, those words wouldn't have cut through me like the north wind. I didn't think I could bear to lose someone else close so soon.

I looked around me and wondered what I would do when my father passed away. He had been right about the work. I was beginning to see that it would be too much for me. Ever since I had returned, I was doing more and more of the chores. It was too much for my father to do all by himself. I wondered how he had managed on his own while I had been away. He must have pushed himself.

If we were in the house at noon, we watched the farm report on the local television station. Every day at 12:10 they covered the markets for grain, livestock, milk and cheese. Beef had been going up, and it was the talk among farmers. For years, beef prices had languished in the same range. Beef producers made just enough money to get by so that they stayed in the business. Now there were farmers expanding their beef herds. The price of heifers calves had skyrocketed.

Some of the demand was for Black Angus beef. We could look back at our choice of breed now and wished we had chosen Black Angus. Groceries stores and restaurants were pushing their Black Angus Beef but we were committed to Hereford. Still the beef market in general was up. Consumers wanted beef because the Atkins Diet program promoted lots of fat and protein.

So when I turned on the television at 12:10, and discovered that beef had increased for the tenth week in a row, I turned to my father. I decided this was a window of opportunity, a way to raise the issue without offending him by telling him he was getting old.

"Look at that. Have you ever thought maybe we should take advantage of the increase and sell our cows?"

I expected my father to say "no way."

But he didn't. "Prices haven't been this high in years, and it isn't likely that they will stay up for long. Cattle producers are going to start expanding and supply will drive down prices."

Surprised, I listened. He continued, " Or the unthinkable could happen here as it did in England. Mad Cow disease has hit Canada. It is only a matter of time before more than an isolated cow or two comes down with it in the U.S. You know Ruthie, I was thinking the same thing myself the other day. Prices are good. We could still crop the land. With Joe doing all the work, we'd mainly have to manage. When you start working fulltime, you sure aren't going to want to come home and spend your evening feeding and caring for a bunch of cattle."

"So you're not opposed to it then," I asked, wanting to check my understanding of what I had just heard.

"No, I was going to suggest it to you, but I wasn't sure how you'd take it. I was afraid you'd think it was a bad idea, a sign that I was getting old. You seem so attached to the farm and the cows. I'm not suggesting we move off the farm, only that we sell the cattle. We can still keep a few around. We might as well. We're set up. We can sell beef halves to the neighbors, or family. Some people are always interested in buying beef directly from the farmer. They like the feeling of knowing where the beef came from."

"That sounds like a good idea. Part of farming is knowing when to act."

My father agreed. "The mistake most farmers make is they get too greedy. When prices on any commodity go up, they wait and see how far they'll go up. Trouble is what goes up quickly, usually comes down in one big thump. No, I think the time is right. If you're willing to sell them, we should do it now."

"I agree with you Dad," I answered.

"Remember how we used to argue?" he asked with a grin.

"How could I forget?" I answered with a laugh.

"Well, we'll have to look around for something new to argue about it. It keeps me young arguing with you. Well I'll go make some phone calls then. Better not dally. "

He started towards the phone. "On second thought," he started to say.

I thought "Oh, oh".

"Maybe it would be a good idea to sell half today, then half next week. If the price goes up, we can take advantage. If it doesn't, we aren't entirely screwed."

"Okay," I said, relieved. "Sounds good to me."

In a few minutes, my father came back to the kitchen to tell me we'd gotten the price we wanted. The truck would be coming at the end of the week to take them to the feedlot.

The day the cattle were loaded up on the truck, my father and I arose well before sun up to coral the herd into the yard. By 7 AM, I was exhausted. I had chased one rascal calf through the hay field for forty-five minutes before she decided to join the others in the cow yard. She had suddenly put on the brakes while running past the opening one more time, flicked her tail in the air, and then had sauntered in through the gate to join the others like it had been her idea all along. I knew at that moment how much I would miss the cows. I almost couldn't bear the thought. But I wouldn't change my mind now. The pendulum on the grandfather clock had moved through its resting point and was ready to change directions. I would have to follow.

The following week we went through the whole arduous ordeal of loading cattle one more time. We were glad we didn't have to do that again any time soon.

We'd saved out half a dozen young cows, half of them in the size range that a summer on pasture would fatten up so they could be sold. The other half would be having their babies in a few months. The six of them looked forlorn to me in the big lot but when I went down to fill their watering trough and move some hay to the feeding station, I didn't mind the idea that it took only a few minutes to finish up. The sound of livestock could still be heard. It would work out.

Another farming anniversary was coming up, reminding me of all the changes in my life. Springtime was a time of life quickening anyway. It seemed like a good time to take some pride in all the changes my father and I had weathered together. I had been a good student. Charlie and my father had turned me into a farmer. I was proud of that, and I reminded myself, I still am one.

Chapter Nineteen
Sweet Taste of Life

Even without cattle, another of nature's cycles beginning was exciting to me. New life would rise from the ground as it warmed in the sunshine. We would plant, grow and harvest. Then winter would come, and we would rest, and the cycle would begin again.

Somehow spring right around the corner eased Charlie's death. He had gone back to the land. He was part of the cycle of life now.

With the return of spring, the old yearning to find the right person to spend the rest of my life with returned. It was almost as if Charlie's death had made room for someone else.

Where would I find him? It didn't seem possible to find him here on the farm, or even the community. Young men weren't going into farming. Maybe I'd find an eligible bachelor in the teaching field, I mused, although I wasn't sure that would make me happy. I wanted someone who felt the same way about the land that I did. That kind of man was hard to find in today's world. I wanted someone who believed in the miracles of life, not in the miracles of money.

I realized that farming had been to my spiritual life like eating the so-called miracle berry from Africa. After eating this berry-like fruit, everything tastes sweet. I had read about the berry in the *Encyclopedia Britannica* as a young girl and had never forgotten. Now I thought of the farm as my miracle berry. I did not need to look to the supernatural or divine for miracles, though some miracles could be explained no other way. I looked to the world of my farm, and, in the fields, in the sky, in the earth, all around me, I found miracles. Did anyone else feel the same way I did?

I wanted someone who saw each seed as a miracle. I knew seeds were miracles. Conditions have to be skewed far to either side of optimum before the seed will fail in producing a plant exactly like the plant that produced the seed. An acre of field corn is an extraordinary number of miracles, 30,000 or more per acre. There are so many miracles in this life that they blind me. When I look around, I wonder, what is not a miracle?

I felt too that I had everything necessary for happiness. There is world enough right here on this farm, I thought. Sometimes I didn't know if I'd be able to leave. Yet I knew I must. I didn't want to end up like Charlie—left alone, with nothing to do but work. He had felt the weight of being alone.

My father and I talked about the miracles on the farm. He agreed with me. Together we wondered what would happen if everyone chewed the miracle berries. Would people stop buying things at the mall that are just like the things they already own that have only one flaw, that they are not new?

Would people respect Mother Earth by no longer fouling the water, air, and soil with wastes and chemical by-products? Would people want to maintain a pristine environment for the miracles that happen in its deep ocean waters, lakes and rivers, lands that rise to mountains and fall to the seas?

Maybe when we looked up at the sky and saw the universe--the oceans of space with so many mysteries not yet revealed—maybe then we would stop warring and senseless killing.

But while I was soaring with miracles, I was grounded by them too, anchored by principles and values that come from the land. The cycle of life, the renewal of resources, simple pleasures from the common and ordinary, these things I learned from the land.

I'd learned from Charlie that the pleasure of sharing, the excitement of giving, a grateful heart returning the gift of caring received from another, softened the struggle of being human.

I'd learned from my father that it is never too late to take a risk, to go after what makes life worth living.

And I had learned that it didn't take as much as I had once thought to have a good life. I was grateful that I no longer chased goals as ephemeral as soap bubbles, as worthless as counterfeit bills.

I knew I should try to hold onto these thoughts as I made my way.

Early daylight was starting to wake me from sleep. As the season progressed I would awaken at the crack of dawn and feel the need to get out of bed. My father was no longer up before me. The tables had turned.

Today I tried to be quiet so as not to awaken him. I decided to make a batch of homemade bread. The kneading of the dough would soothe me. There was something elemental about combining the flour and the water with the other ingredients and coming up not with floury paste but with this yeasty dough that rose from the warmth of the room. One of the great pleasures in life was biting into a warm slice of bread cut from a loaf fresh out of the oven. I mixed up the dough, then made coffee, and grabbed a warm jacket. I went out to the front porch to watch the sun climb over the fields.

Off in the distance, the hills were starting to change. Yesterday I could see the faintest blush of pink. Today, more red had crept into the pink, a touch of yellow. It wouldn't be long and Joe would be plowing and planting. I breathed deep of the clean fresh air. I liked this time, when the air was still raw from winter, but softening from spring's emerging touch. I glanced at my watch. Almost an hour had passed. I better go check on the bread.

Inside, I punched down the dough and moved the pan closer to the sunlight. There was no worry about chores. I would go down after another cup of coffee and water and feed the cattle.

After another cup, I slipped outside and made my way down to the cow yard. With so few around, they were getting tamer. I petted my favorite on her head, and she nuzzled me back. I called her "Little Red." My father was warning me not to get too attached. "She going to end up on your dinner plate, and then what will you do?"

I argued back that I could make her a pet if I wanted. I pointed out that old Hank down the road had an old bull that he called Jester. He'd had Jester for fifteen years and he was Hank's pet. Hank fed her, watered her, and talked to her. People laughed at Hank and his Jester, but I understood how he felt.

"Well, we aren't going to do that, Ruthie," my father warned.

Then we'd be off and running on an argument.

"I guess we've found something to argue about, Ruthie," my father would say after awhile. "Keep it up, you're going to keep me young."

Just then I heard a truck pull in. I half expected it to be Joe. He stopped here often. He liked to talk to my father about farming. He and my father had become good friends. Joe had been in agreement about selling the cattle. He said we wouldn't see prices this good for many years to come. Now he was trying to persuade my father to come work for him. If I knew my father, he would be driving one of Joe's big pieces of equipment as soon as the ground could be worked.

But when I saw the truck, it wasn't Joe. I watched the man climb down. At first I didn't recognize him. He was tall, graying at the temples, but walked with a purposeful and sure stride towards me. He was carrying something in his arms. His face was familiar but it took me a second to place him.

Jim Phillips, the man I had met the night Charlie died. I had last seen him at the funeral home. He had a pleasant way about him, I thought as I looked at him. He was wearing a heartfelt smile, his eyes watching my face for a sign that I welcomed his visit. I saw that he was carrying two gray cardboard cartons of eggs.

He thrust the eggs in my direction. "I brought you some farm fresh eggs. I thought maybe you and your father would enjoy them. They're fresh today. I can't eat all the eggs my hens want to lay."

I stood there. I think my mouth had fallen open in surprise. I stammered out, "Thank you." Then I remembered my manners. "Would you like to come in and have a cup of coffee?"

"No need for that," he answered.

I opened the carton to look at the eggs. Inside the gray box were eggs in every shade of brown, from burnt umber to sienna to ochre. Some were almost as big as ostrich eggs. Some as small as quail eggs. I put out my finger and touched their hard surface. These eggs seemed like beautiful porcelain china pieces.

I looked at Jim, my face beaming with pleasure, and said sincerely, "Thank you for the wonderful eggs. It makes me want to have my own chickens. They are so beautiful."

"Oh, I have plenty of eggs, enough to share with you," he said. "To be honest, I really came over to see if would care to join me for dinner tonight? I thought we could have a nice steak, a piece of pie, a cup of coffee. Just a friendly dinner, maybe we can talk about farming, things we have in common. I know you don't know me at all, but there is only one way to fix that. What do you say?"

I heard something, a sound like the sweet sound of a bluebird singing. There was something about Jim Phillips that reminded me somehow of Charlie.

I looked at his hands, big, strong hands, dangling from his empty arms. He was wearing a clean jacket, but it was obviously a work jacket, frayed on the cuffs, work gloves stuffed in the pockets. He was lean, fit, and happy.

I said, "What time?"

"How about six?" he answered.

"That sounds fine," I replied, smiling back at him.

"We'll go to the Black Bear. Ever been there?"

I shook my head.

"Oh you'll like it. They have a great big stone fireplace with a cozy fire, the best steak you've ever tasted, and wonderful service. It's a quiet place, elegant I'd say. The rowdy crowd stays away. We'll be able to talk to each other without shouting to be heard."

"I should dress up then?" I asked.

"Oh, you'll be fine no matter what you wear. But if you want to, that'll be okay. If you don't, that'll be okay too."

He stood there for a minute grinning at me with delight. "I'll pick you up at six then?"

I nodded agreement.   He turned and walked away.

I watched him go to his truck, climb up with one big sure stride and then when he had driven off, I continued to stand there under the bare tree holding the eggs in my arms, still overcome by surprise, as the sun climbed higher to greet what promised to be a perfect spring day. Finally I roused myself. I started to move towards the house so I could put the eggs in the refrigerator.

Suddenly the sky darkened slightly. I looked up, afraid that clouds were moving in. I heard a familiar sound in the air. I tilted my head back and there above me was a flock of swans, headed north. I worried for a moment that they were hesitating, remembering Lake Charlie, but this year we had no great pools of water lying on the land. This year we were having a normal spring.

I stood in awe as the flock flew overhead, past Lake Charlie, past our farm, their graceful bodies silhouetted against the cerulean sky, their honking clearly audible as they made their way to places far away where I had never been but that someday I hoped to see.

Then the back door opened and my father stuck his head out the door.

"Ruthie, why are you standing out there with two cartons of eggs in your hand?"

I hurried towards him, careful that I did not drop the eggs in my rush to tell him all the events that had already happened on this day.

About the Author

Candace Hennekens is the author of three non-fiction books: *Healing Your Life: Recovery from Domestic Abuse, Yes to Career Success! For Women in Transition*, and *There's a Rainbow in my Glass of Lemonade.*

Sweet Farm of Mine is the first book in a series written about the author's experiences as a farmer. The sequel to this book is *Sweet Land of Mine,* which tells more about Ruthie's journey.

Hennekens also has written a book of poetry, a book of short stories, and other novels set in the Midwestern landscape. Visit her website at candacehennekens.com to learn more, including her life as an artist.

***

www.ingramcontent.com/pod-product-compliance
Lightning Source LLC
Chambersburg PA
CBHW060804120626
46557CB00001B/83